Allison Burnett
Undiscovered Gyrl

Allison Burnett is the author of *Christopher*, a
finalist for the 2004 PEN Center USA Literary
Award, and *The House Beautiful*.

ALSO BY ALLISON BURNETT

Christopher

The House Beautiful

Undiscovered Gyrl

Undiscovered Gyrl

a novel

Allison Burnett

VINTAGE CONTEMPORARIES
Vintage Books
A Division of Random House, Inc.
New York

A VINTAGE CONTEMPORARIES ORIGINAL, AUGUST 2009

Copyright © 2009 by Allison Burnett

All rights reserved. Published in the United States by Vintage Books,
a division of Random House, Inc., New York, and in Canada by Random House
of Canada Limited, Toronto.

Vintage and colophon are registered trademarks and Vintage Contemporaries
is a trademark of Random House, Inc.

Library of Congress Cataloging-in-Publication Data
Burnett, Allison.
    Undiscovered gyrl : a novel / by Allison Burnett.
        p. cm.—(Vintage contemporaries)
    ISBN 978-0-307-47312-7
    1. Teenage girls—Fiction.   2. Blogs—Fiction.   I. Title.
    PS3602.U763U63 2009
    813'.6—dc22   2009006812

Book design by Debbie Glasserman

www.vintagebooks.com

Printed in the United States of America
10 9 8 7 6 5 4 3 2 1

For darling Chloe

"After all, life hasn't much to offer except youth and I suppose for older people the love of youth in others."

— F. SCOTT FITZGERALD

Undiscovered Gyrl

Thursday, October 25, 2007

Last April when I decided to defer college for a year my friends said I was insane, but I'm not. I have no idea what I want to do with my life. What a waste of time and money to go to college if you don't know. My mom was furious at me when I told her, although she pretended she wasn't. She said "But, sweetheart, that's what college is for. To discover your bliss." That sounds great on paper but what if I don't discover my bliss until the end of sophomore year and it has nothing to do with the classes I've already taken? I'd have to start over. Or what if it turns out my bliss is something that doesn't require a college degree? Like jewelry design. Or horseback riding. Or sex. Ha!

The next morning my mother emailed me and said if I was really serious about deferring and wanted to go on living at home, I'd have to get a full-time job. What did she think I was going to do, hang around the house all day?

When I told my English teacher, Ms. Rath, of my decision, she took off her hippie glasses, rubbed the purple spots on both sides of her big-pored nose and said "I'm concerned. A

girl like you needs structure." As if you can only get structure at college! That's pretty harsh to all the kids who can't
afford to go. And what about the girls who do go but instead
of studying get drunk every night and bone the whole football team? Is that structure? Ms. Rath said I should keep a
journal or start a blog so that one day I will look back on my
year off and learn from the experience. I told her that was a
wonderful idea. I was lying to get away from her yellow
teeth and vegan breath. At least that's what I thought at the
time. Guess not!

I hope I'm not a disgrace at blogging. I have always excelled
at creative writing but I suck at grammar and punctuation
and can barely write my own name without spell-check.
(Ms. Rath thinks I'm mildly slysdexic. Ha!) Maybe this
experiment will help me to discover my bliss faster. Hope
so. Bye.

Wednesday, October 31, 2007
Most blogs are just some boring chick telling you everything you never wanted to know about her stupid life.
Every single day she tells you more boring details until
you just want to write to her and say "Yo, bitch, when something actually happens, let me know!" My blog will be the
exact opposite. I'll only write when I have something fasci-

nating to report. Which is not now. Right now it's Halloween. I'm going to put on my rotting corpse mask and get drunk.

Friday, November 2, 2007

Last night Dan called and asked if I wanted to come over and watch a movie. We both know what that means. Which is why I swore I'd never go back. But I did. In fact I ran the whole way. I have no will power. Outside his front door I put on my corpse mask and when he opened up I screamed "Boo!" He wasn't scared at all. He just laughed.

It's always the same with me and Dan. As soon as I get to his house, we light up cigarettes and start bitching about our love lives. Last night I complained about how when I got home really late Saturday night from a semi-rave, my boyfriend Rory was waiting outside my house. He flipped out and called me "a disgusting whore" even though I hadn't done anything wrong. All I did was drink rum and root beers with a really funny skate-rat named Tobias who's gay and doesn't know it yet. Rory didn't believe me. He got so jealous he yelled in my face and shook the shit out of me. When I told him to get the fuck out and never come back, he panicked. Within two minutes he was whining like a little bitch, telling me how much he loved me and begging me not to break up. He is grotesquely insecure. I have to dump him.

Now it was Dan's turn. He complained about his French girlfriend, Martine, and how she's been getting crazier and crazier lately. Right before her period, she calls him terrible names and throws heavy objects at his head. He says that at these times she is "unfit for human consumption." They had a major fight this week because he wants her to go on Prozac a few days before each period and she said no way, she's not some stupid American who takes a pill every time she has an emotion.

Now that we've finished justifying what's about to occur, Dan gets out the weed and I pick out a film from the three he's Netflicked. Dan teaches cinema studies at a local college. He is absolutely brilliant and is writing his P.H.D. on Anti-Americanism in the works of Jean Luc Godard. The movies he picks for us to watch are all classics. No Hollywood junk. My relationship with Dan would be like my own personal film school if only I could get through a single movie with my pants on. Hahaha!

Last night it was so cold out that while Dan stuffed the bong, I borrowed one of his sweaters. I chose a big gray cashmere V-neck with holes in the armpits. Older men's sweaters are the best. ☺

. . .

We got totally stoned off two hits each then Dan hit play. The film was "The Seven Beauties" by Lena Vertmuller. (She also directed the incredible "Swept Away" which most people think is about sex but is actually about the class system in Italian society.) As usual we sat on opposite sides of the couch. Then about 15 minutes later, also as usual, I crawled over, pushed him down on his back and laid my head on his chest. I love watching movies like this, even though I can barely hear the dialogue sometimes, because of the noise his hand makes as he gently scratches my scalp. A therapist would say it's because I get no love from my dad. I say so what? It still feels amazing.

I lose track of time on marijuana so I never know exactly how long it is before I kiss him. But I'm always the one who kisses first. If Dan made the first move he would feel way too guilty. He's 32 and I'm 17. Can you say "jailbait"?

Once we start kissing, Dan goes insane. He pulls my shirt up, grinds me to death and in about two minutes my pants and underwear are on the floor. Is every older guy a master at oral sex or just Dan? I guess I'll find out one day. Can't wait!

Besides how good it feels, I also love it because I get to close my eyes and let my stoned mind wander wherever it wants to. A real journey. Last night I was back in our old house before my dad moved out. We were watching the

Greenbay Packers on TV. When he screamed at the TV so did I, even though I was only six years old and didn't understand the rules. Then I was floating on my back in a perfectly clear lake where we used to go every summer and the sunny sky had no clouds and Mr. Silaggi, the Hungarian man with the cabin next to ours, was on the shore clapping for me because it was the first time I'd ever floated with no help. He was wearing plaid shorts with black socks to cover the earthworm veins in his calves. Then it was last June and Principal Wise was handing me my diploma and whispering "We're all so proud of you, Katherine." He said this because as a freshman I spent three days in a mental hospital. Instead of his kind compliment making me feel good, it made me feel sorry for myself because it reminded me that my dad was too sick and selfish to be there. And then all of the sudden I was back in the present and Dan was crawling up my stomach wiping his mouth and saying "You get so close. Every time. But you always hold back."

"I'm sorry."

"Don't be sorry. It's your loss not mine."

Sad but true!

One wonderful thing about hooking up with an older guy is that you don't have to reciprocate. Younger guys practically grab you by the hair and push you onto their dicks. "My turn!" Or else if they're the sensitive type, they tell you how making love will bring you so much closer, and then they start to whine and beg like a puppy. Yuck! Dan never makes demands. The only way I even knew I was sexually frustrating him is that one time at the door he said "I'm going to cum before you get to the corner." He was joking of course but I got the point. The reason I've been so selfish with him is that I always thought if we did anything more, we would end up having sex. I've never slept with a guy older than 22. Will it be different? Will I hate it? Or will I love it so much I'll never want to have sex with a guy my own age again? These are the questions I ask.

Anyway, last night lying on the couch with the charming sound of Italian coming from the TV, Dan told me some really bad news. He's moving away. Not that far but too far to walk. And since there's no bus in that direction, I would need a car to get there, which I don't have. Yes, of course, Dan could pick me up but I know he won't. I don't really blame him. It's one thing to hook up with an underage girl when she runs over to your house and leaves pretty soon after it's over. It's totally different to drive 30 minutes to pick her up, then take her all the way back to your place, fool around and drive her all the way home again. It's much sleazier.

I told Dan I hated that we're never going to see each other again all because of a stupid fucking car. He said "Don't be ridiculous. Of course we'll see each other. Just not as much." He hated to see me cry. He started kissing my neck, my cheeks, my nose, my mouth. I don't know why I did it—

maybe because I was missing him already—but I broke my rule. I unbuttoned his jeans and slipped my hand inside, over his boxers. He was unbelievably hard. You should have seen his face when I started pulling. Like he was seeing god! But the sounds he made were the exact opposite, like he was being tortured alive. I always thought if we did something like this it would instantly turn to sex but it didn't. He was content with what he was getting and didn't try for more. After he came, he just laid there sopping wet, smiling his ass off. He said "Thanks for the box job" and we both laughed.

Our dates always end with junk food. Last night it was popcorn, string cheese, caramel ice cream and baby carrots. I drank three beers pretty fast which got Dan going on his favorite lecture. He said I was flirting with alcoholism and that unless I quit drinking I am on my way to a shit life. I replied all bored and sophisticated like Betty Davis, blowing smoke from my cigarette.

I said "Oh, dahling, you really must find a new subject. This one is so dreary!"

He didn't even smile.

He said "Your drinking is fun and exciting now because you're young and beautiful but when you're thirty it's just going to be pathetic."

I pretended to be overjoyed. "Seriously? You think I'm beautiful?"

"Stop joking around! This is important!"

I told him he was totally wrong and that I love alcohol way too much to ever let myself get addicted to it and have to quit. This made him laugh.

When Dan and I first met, I told him all about my dad. How two years ago he almost died of a heart attack. What I didn't tell him was that this occurred right after my dad had surgery to remove like half his stomach because of ulcers he made worse by his horrendous drinking. If Dan knew my father was a boozer, he would know alcoholism runs in my family and that he was right to worry about my excessive drinking. This would be totally humiliating. The only thing bad about going out with older guys is that they're almost always right. Grrrrrr.

Maybe the pot was stronger than usual or maybe the box job was too much for the old dude, but when I got back from the bathroom he was sound asleep. He looked pretty cute lying there. At first I was just going to tuck him in and leave but I was sleepy too. So I squished in next to him and closed my eyes. When I opened them it was morning. Dan was snoring softly with his hand up my shirt, cupping my boob. Birds were singing outside. I thought about Rory and felt guilty.

Thank god I didn't stop for coffee on the way home, because right after I got back, Rory knocked on my bedroom door, which means if I'd stopped for coffee, Rory would have found my room empty and known I'd slept out. The only person whose house I ever sleep over at (besides his) is my best friend Jade's, but she's visiting her grandma in Thailand right now. So Rory would have known I was with another guy and I would now be dead.

"I can't believe you're awake so early," he said. "I was going to crawl in bed with you."

"My mom and I had a huge brawl last night. I couldn't sleep."

"Hey, what's up with your lip?"

I didn't even have to look in the mirror to know what he was talking about. Whenever I hook up with Dan his beard scratches the shit out of my top lip. (Dan is half Italian and has manly stubble. Rory is all Irish and barely has pubes.) How could I explain the redness? I was so scared! I was in no mood to be abused.

"Photo-dermabrasion," I said.

"Never heard of it."

"It's a laser process that removes broken blood vessels and unwanted moles and freckles from your face. Didn't I tell you I got it done?"

The only reason I know about the procedure is that last week I got my teeth cleaned and there was an Allure magazine in the waiting room.

"I think I'd remember. When did you get it done?"

"Tuesday. My dermatologist gave me a free sample. Just

for like a minute. Remember that little mole I had? It's gone now. See?"

Rory inspected my lip and yup the mole was gone but only because I never had one. Ha!

"Does it hurt?" he asked. "It looks all scraped."

"A little. But in a few days I'll look awesome."

"You mean even hotter?"

"Hard to believe, huh?"

"Impossible."

We laughed and fell on the bed.

Our sex would have been so much better if I hadn't been thinking the whole time how I hadn't showered yet and how lucky I was that Rory didn't notice I was wearing a huge men's sweater.

Such a long post! It took me four hours to write, most of which was spent spell-checking. Hahaha! I'm serious. I wonder if all my posts will be this long or if it's just because it's all so new and exciting? When I was 11, I kept a diary and I wrote in it every single day for a month. Then I stopped forever. I hope I don't do that again. I quit too many things. The only things I don't quit are the things I should: drinking, smoking and Rory. Ha!

I'm sad about Dan moving away. I never really thought I was in love with him but maybe I am. I can't stop thinking about last night and the sounds and faces he made when I touched him. My heart aches at the thought that I might not ever kiss his mouth or hold him close again. Must sleep.

Saturday, November 3, 2007

Yesterday morning when I was leaving Dan's I said "Since this might be the last time we ever see each other, don't you want to walk me home?"

He replied "Nope, but I'll tell you what, if you get attacked on the way home and the guy isn't cute, scream and I'll come save you."

I frowned like I was really offended by the rape joke and stormed away. But when I got to the sidewalk I spun around with a big smile. Dan was so relieved I wasn't pissed! Seeing him standing there smiling, so sexy in his crusty boxers with his strong legs, big chest and messed-up hair, I really didn't want to go, so I ran back and gave him the sexiest, most delicious kiss ever. At the same time I stroked my hand up his thigh.

You should have seen his face.

Then I ran away.

Katie Kampenfelt strikes again! Ha!

Monday, November 5, 2007

I got an email today from julietisdead who is positive that I'm some slut from her high school named Katie Loomis who goes out with a football player named Rory McGirk. Sorry, babe, I've never been to Arkansas and no way would I ever date a jock. I prefer brains over brawn. Besides, Rory isn't in high school. He's a senior at the college where Dan teaches.

Just so you know, if I thought there was even a one in a google chance of anyone recognizing me from this blog, I would never ever be this honest. And what's the point of blogging if you're not going to tell the truth?

The reason I'll never be recognized is that I've changed every single name including my own. I have also changed many random meaningless details. For example, Dan lives in an apartment not a house. My dad did not have a heart attack after his operation. He caught a staph infection. (Just as bad.) And Jade's grandmother does not live in Thailand. She lives in the Philippines. You get the idea.

All the important details are accurate.

Budburkel7 wants to know why I was in a mental hospital for three days when I was 13. Well, Bud, old pal, it's because the summer before I started high school I was totally out of control. I was angry and rebellious, failed to show up for computer camp, and was always sneaking out my bedroom window at night. One day after my mom and I had a huge fight, I stole a bunch of her Ambien and some cash and ran away to live with a lifeguard I had a massive crush on. When he told me to go home I started crying hysterically and locked myself in his dirty bathroom. He called 911. When the cops arrived I refused to open the door so they had to bust it down. After I got out of the psych ward, I was required to see a shrink four times a week for the rest of the summer. We argued constantly. He thought most of my problems had to do with my parents' hideous divorce. I thought that was too easy.

That's interesting, bridgetLK. I had no idea that titles of movies, magazines, books and TV shows were supposed to be in italics. You're positive, right? I'm not even sure how to make them!

Tuesday, November 6, 2007

I've been out of school for five months now and I still haven't found a full-time job, this is mostly due to the fact that I have never looked for one. Why, you ask? Why have I not looked when I promised my mom that I would? Well, first I graduated from high school and I wanted to have fun with my friends before they left for pre-college vacations or started boring office jobs in the city, then I met Rory on the Fourth of July and thought I was in love. Since I still had some money left over from the $5,000 my grandma left me when she died (she left the rest to the Catholic Church to pay their molester bills), I decided to take it easy until the end of summer when I would begin life as a responsible adult. But by the time Labor Day came, I was in the habit of being a lazy loser, and then I met Dan, which was another thing to distract me.

Anyway I'm now broke off my ass and my mom says she's going to kick me out December first unless I start "fending for myself." She wouldn't really do it, of course. I am the light of her life. But she's right. It's time to get serious.

I would have gone job hunting today only I have terrible PMS. I'm not like Dan's girlfriend, Martine, who turns into the devil incarnated every month. I just get very, very sad. For example tonight I started sobbing during *Dancing with the Stars* (italics!) even though it's the most heinous and appalling program in the history of television. Then I missed Dan so badly I talked to Rory on the phone for almost two hours. He wanted to come over but I said no. I'm about to break out on my chin. The last thing I want is sex.

I have very few friends these days. Rory and Jade are basically it. My friends who are away at college hardly ever email or text anymore. It's natural that people grow apart once college starts but when it happens this fast, you've got to think maybe you weren't that close in the first place. A lot of it's my fault. Often my sense of humor gets out of control and I hurt people's feelings. Worst of all is my power over guys. When my friends and I go out, I am always the one guys talk to. It's not just my looks. It's everything. I know how to get guys to like me. It's been my genius since I was little. It makes my friends insanely jealous. I don't blame them. I'd hate to be in their unloved shoes. But what am I supposed to do? Gain weight, stop showering and act like a dyke just so they can get some play? The only reason Jade has stayed my friend is because she's as hot as I am and the guys she's attracted to are not my type and vice versa.

Wednesday, November 7, 2007

I felt like killing myself all day. Now I am too sleepy to do it.

Thursday, November 8, 2007

Dan moved today. He called to say goodbye but I was still asleep. When I listened to his voice mail, I started bawling. Is it because I'm in love with him or is it just hormones? A deep and difficult mystery for a gyrl to answer. Probably some of both. I'm hungry. I wish I had a car. Boo hoo!

Friday, November 9, 2007

This morning as I was leaving to job hunt, my mom's boy-friend Mark Aubichon said "Good luck finding a job, hot-shot. And if you do, good luck earning more than minimum wage." He's always telling me how shitty my life is going to be unless I do exactly what he thinks I should do. Right now he believes that me deferring college was supremely dumb.

"Thanks for the support," I said. "I'm touched."

He patted the egg yolk off his ugly mouth. Not only is he a negative arrogant person but he has no neck. He looks exactly like a bullfrog with a mustache. And hairy knuckles.

He replied "Facts are facts. Without a college degree, be prepared to work like a slave for the rest of your life for very little compensation."

I squinted at him with hate. "You underestimate my pow-ers, earthling."

My mom laughed and said "You've got to love my kid's confidence!"

"No I don't," Mark replied, chewing turkey sausage with his mouth open. Smack, smack, smack.

At the door I turned around and said "If you're right and my life sucks, I'll just have to marry an ugly, old billionaire. The first time he sees me naked, which will be on our hon-eymoon, he'll have a heart attack and die. I'll inherit his entire fortune. You can be my chauffeur."

Door slam.

Walking down the alley I could still hear my mother laughing inside. She loves when I give Mark shit. Maybe because she's such a doormat.

Once I entered the house late at night and overheard Mark and my mom having sex by the fireplace. She was moaning like she was flying on a magic carpet. I almost puked into the kitchen sink. I would give anything for her to dump him. Jade's mom says it will never happen because women over 45 have a better chance of getting blown up by a terrorist than finding a man. Haha! If I ever get that desperate, I will buy a giant vibrator and never leave the house.

By the time I reached Main Street I was dripping sweat. Just my luck I didn't bring sunblock and I was too broke to buy any. I walked around for like two hours, stopping at every halfway decent store to see if they were hiring. They weren't, so I tried the lame stores. The managers were all really nice to me, especially the guys, but what could they do? You can't invent a job if there isn't one.

I started thinking "Oh man, what if Mark Aubichon is right? What if all I can get is some fast-food job and when everybody comes home for Christmas break they see me sitting in the drive-through window? I'll be a laughing stock!" I imagined them holding up their phones as they drove by, taking pics to post online.

I got so depressed I started thinking maybe it was good

that it was so hot out in November. Maybe we deserve global warming. It will put mankind out of its misery. I pictured the planet with everything baked to death. Nothing left but miles and miles of sand and thousands of camels. I imagined their funny faces and silly humps and that made me feel better.

Just when I was ready to text Rory and order him to buy me lunch, I saw a big burly man standing inside the front window of the Corner Store, taping up a help wanted poster. I ran over and screamed "Hold it right there, mister! I'm just the girl for you!" Pretty stupid considering I didn't even know what the job was. But I knew he would think it was adorable. He smiled and waved for me to hold on. As he climbed out of the window, I could see his butt crack and that the store had totally changed inside. All the cute gifts were gone and there were piles and piles of old books. When he came outside I was nervous, maybe because I knew I looked like shit, all sweaty and sunburned. I started blabbering about how when I was a little girl I bought all my Christmas presents at the Corner Store and that I had no idea it was closing.

He said "Well, I hate to be the bearer of bad news, but John died of prostate cancer a few months ago."

"Oh, no! That's so sad!"

I had no idea which of the two gray-haired homos was John but either way it was sad because they were both extremely nice.

"Lee sold me the place a couple of months ago and moved to Arizona."

"What's it going to be now?"

"Elysium Used and Rare Books."

"Awesome."

"Are you a bibliophile?"

"A what?"

"Book lover."

"Oh, yeah. Definitely. I adore reading."

He smiled like he knew I was lying. Wouldn't that be the worst? A boss who could tell every time you were lying? The only thing worse would be a boyfriend who could tell.

"Well, I used to," I explained. "Lately not so much. Too many distractions. You know, being a teenager and everything."

I gave him my sweetest smile. I could tell he liked me. He reached out a giant hand.

"Glenn Warburg."

"Katie Kampenfelt."

I gave him a good firm shake. My dad says this is essential if you want men to respect you.

Glenn Warburg isn't the kind of person you would picture owning a book store. He looks more like a retired cop. He's tall with a big balding head, semi-potbelly, heavy legs and acne scars on his cheeks. I'm not sure how he usually dresses but today he was wearing a red sweatshirt, acid-washed jeans and big brown boots. His only nice features are his perfect white smile and twinkly blue eyes. He also wears a diamond post in his ear, which makes no sense, as he is not the gay or groovy type. He just moved here from Chicago. Since most of his business is online, he figured why pay big city rent? Standing outside on the sidewalk he told me all about the job except the most important thing.

"How much does it pay?" I asked.

"I don't know. What's the going rate around here?"

"I get fifteen an hour to babysit."

This was technically true. The one and only time I ever babysat that's what I made. It was just this past summer. My mom's best friend Cynthia Crowder was visiting from Atlanta. Her son Chase didn't really need a sitter because he's in junior high, but Cynthia knew I was going broke fast.

"How about twelve?" Glenn said.

"Off the books?"

"Sure."

"How many hours a week?"

"I don't know. A minimum of thirty. Maximum of forty. Make your own schedule. Start Monday."

Done! Not even an application. For all he knows I could be an illegal alien. From Sweden. Ha! And the best part of all is that the job is butt-easy. All I do is help customers out front while Glenn's in back working on his computer. When there's no customers, I'm in charge of shipping books. When there's no books to ship, I can do anything I want. Or as Glenn put it, "You're free to get lost in the stacks." Stacks must mean shelves. Anybody know for sure?

You should have seen the look on Mark Aubichon's face when I told him my good news. His eyes bugged out like he'd swallowed a horsefly. Ha! My mom tried not to laugh. How pathetic that he couldn't just say congratulations. Instead he started asking me all these questions about Glenn, like he didn't believe he really existed. Like I'd made the whole thing up! What a sore loser. Lawyers suck. They'd rather die than be wrong.

Once I convinced him Glenn was real, Mark thought for a second then asked me if he was married.

"I find that question really insulting."

"Why?"

"You think the only way I could get a job this good is because of how I look. You think Glenn wants to bone me. That is so sexist. He happens to think I'm brilliant!"

I shoved back my chair and threw down my napkin. I wasn't really pissed at all. It's just that my mom hates it when I leave the table early and I wanted to IM Jade in Manila before her day started.

. . .

I wonder if working around books all day will get me inspired about learning so that I will want to go to college next year? Sure hope so. Good night!

Oh, I asked Glenn what Elysium means. He said it's the ancient Greek version of heaven, a beautiful happy place where good people go after they die. He said he named his shop Elysium because when you disappear into a great book that's as close to heaven as life gets.

Monday, November 12, 2007

Even though Veterans Day was yesterday, it was officially celebrated today. Most stores were closed but Glenn said he had no choice but to open up, because his flyers were already printed and they said today was the grand opening. He predicted that we would still get many customers and he was right. Unfortunately we weren't fully ready for them. There were a lot of books still in boxes and the credit card machine didn't work.

"Grand openings never run smoothly," Glenn said.

When things finally slowed down around 3:00, we ate yummy fattening deli sandwiches in the back room. (I had corn beef and he had egg salad. He's a vegetarian.) Glenn did most of the talking, not because I was shy or anything

but because I love listening to him so much. He's so fucking smart. He told me all about a writer named Norman
Mailer who died recently. He called him a "hardworking
brilliant buffoon" who wrote "one very good novel about
war and fifty other books about himself." Then since he
mentioned war, I asked him about Veterans Day and what it
meant.

He explained that Veterans Day was created at the end of
World War One, the worst, most tragic, bloodiest war ever,
which ended on the eleventh hour of the eleventh day of the
eleventh month in 1918. Glenn says what most people don't
know is that when the sun rose on that last morning, even
though all the officers knew the war would be officially over
at eleven o'clock, many decided to go right on fighting until
the deadline. Some did it because orders are orders. Others
did it hoping for last-minute medals. And others did it,
believe it or not, because they didn't want to lug all those
heavy bombs back to headquarters. I know, I know! I
couldn't believe it either. Anyway, guess how many soldiers
were wounded or died that last morning? Eleven thousand.
Creepy, right? Can you imagine being the mother or father
of one of those soldiers who died that last morning for nothing? I'd be so mad, I'd probably go berserk and kill a general
with my bare hands.

I liked learning this because Veterans Day has never
meant anything to me. I don't know a single person in the
army. Glenn knows four soldiers in Iraq right now and one

in Afghanistan. Three are sons of old friends and one is a customer's daughter.

Walking home I was really happy not only because I have a wonderful new job but also because it was cold out and I could finally smell winter. Just thinking about Christmas makes me want to cry with joy. It reminds me of being a little girl. Of the time before my mom kicked my dad out, back when I thought we were a happy family. He moved out a week before Christmas, the day after my seventh birthday party. What's weird is that I have a genius memory and remember many things from when I was just a baby, but I have no memory at all of him leaving. I hope we get snow early this year.

All the way home I couldn't stop thinking about Dan and how much he would love what Glenn taught me about World War One. You should see how many books Dan has in his apartment. The first time I came over I said "Have you actually read all these or are they just to impress people? He replied "Both." At least he's honest.

Dan would be so proud I'm working in a bookstore. Once we were watching a brilliant film called *All About Eve*, which is about Broadway theater people and I said that maybe I would become an actress one day and he said "Don't even joke. You have way too good a mind to waste it."

I squeezed one of my boobs and made a cheesy *Maxim* pose and said "But what about my body? Wouldn't it be a shame to waste this too?"

He said "Beauty's commonplace. Intelligence isn't."

A pretty big compliment, right? I think so.

I feel like calling Dan right now and telling him that before we officially never see each other again we should make love. Just once. How could he refuse that? Impossible.

Knock on my door. Somebody bothering me. Stand by.

LATER: 11:58 p.m.

I'm so disgusted. It's one thing to enjoy a bad movie because you know it's bad and another to enjoy it because you actually think it's good. Rory brought over a movie tonight that was awful to the extreme, like it was written by a retarded man on the toilet. I already forget what it's called, but it starred Adam Sandler. Rory loved every asinine minute of it! Watching him laugh his ass off while he crammed cheese popcorn in his mouth made me hate everything about him. I could not believe I had ever made love to this red-haired dope. Usually I think his freckles are adorable, but tonight they looked like giant flakes of fish food. Thank god he brought some beer with him, because it was the only way I got through it without strangling him.

As soon as it was over, I kicked his ass out. He couldn't

understand why I was being such a bitch. He was baffled and bewildered. I told him that I am a mysterious gyrl. That's the problem with dating somebody you're not truly in love with. Every few weeks the pressure builds and you turn into a monster. You're not sure who you hate more for the lie you are living, him or yourself.

Dan says people who cheat these days almost always get caught off their cell phones or cell phone bills. He says it's the modern-day version of lipstick on the collar or the motel receipt in the pocket. That's why I'm not allowed to call him ever. And I can only email if absolutely necessary. He's afraid Martine will be looking over his shoulder when it arrives.

"Just tell her I'm one of your students," I said.

"Too risky," he replied. "She's paranoid by nature."

I'm going to email him right now and tell him I found a great job but I won't say what it is. (Just so he'll know I'm not trying to get him in trouble, I'll write "your last lecture" in the subject line.) Maybe he'll be so curious to know what my new job is, he'll write back or call.

Just sent it. 12 seconds ago. No answer yet. Hahaha!

My whole life, my father promised to buy me a car when I turn 18. That's 33 days away. If my dad ever kept his word, I would soon be able to drive over and see Dan whenever he wanted. How amazing would that be? With my new job and Jade getting back from Manila soon, I would have the ideal life.

Tuesday, November 13, 2007

No call or email from Dan yet but I did get a voice message from a kid named Joel Seidler who was two years ahead of me in school. (When I was a sophomore, he was my geometry tutor. After he went off to Princeton, I never saw him again.) The message he left was friendly but weirdly intense. He always had a crush on me but he never told me about it because he assumed I would never like him back. He assumed right. Joel is scrawny with a gigantic nose, big black-ringed eyes and hips wider than his shoulders. Oh, and he's bow-legged. Next!

On the other hand, Joel is really smart and funny and loves to talk about serious things. He's back from college for some reason and wants to hang out with me. I would love to see him but if Rory found out, he would go ballistic. It's not worth the stress. I swear, there is no worse quality in a guy than excessive jealousy. Except maybe cheapness. Rory is cheap too.

I've only been writing this blog for like three weeks but according to my tracking site it gets between 450 and 500 discrete visitors a day. Is this good? Sure seems like it. I wonder who the hell you all are. The most popular blog search terms that lead you to me are gyrl, high school, sex, oral sex and bliss.

If you guys want me to answer your emails, please stop calling me names. I'm not proud of cheating on Rory. And normally I would never mess around with a guy who has a girlfriend. I had no idea Martine even existed until after the third time Dan and I fooled around, when I found a brand-new box of tampons under his sink. I got really mad and asked why he didn't tell me. He said because they were going to break up any minute. When I left that night I was positive I wasn't coming back. But I couldn't do it. I already liked him too much. I was hooked. If that makes me a slut, too bad.

I got 12 emails this week asking me to send a pic of myself. They were all from guys, except one from a black lesbian in the Air Force. Because she is risking her life for our country I emailed her a topless self-pic of me. No face, of course. She can tape it to her cockpit and try not to crash. Ha! As for everyone else, use your imaginations.

Wednesday, November 14, 2007
Last night I went to this college bar to eat stale peanuts, drink watery beer and listen to Rory's band, Epiphany

Cream Assassin. Between songs I went to pee and not even planning it, I walked right past the bathroom door and into the back alley and called Dan. I know, desperate, dumb, drunk and deviant. Well, guess what? Martine answered. I'm serious. I was so surprised, I couldn't think of a single thing to say.

She said "Allo, Allo, who is zees? Allo?"

I hung up in her face, which was the stupidest thing I could have done. I should have just pretended it was a wrong number. If she told Dan about the call I'm already dead because my mom's name comes up on Caller ID. (She pays my phone bill.) When I got back to the table I must have looked like I'd smoked crack in the bathroom or something, because all the other band girlfriends asked me what was wrong.

I replied "Not drunk enough."

They laughed and poured. By the time the gig was over I was totally shit-faced. I was so sure Dan would never speak to me again that I was really grateful to have a boyfriend, even if it was only Rory. I dragged him back to my house, ripped his clothes off, and sat on him without a condom. I told him it was a safe time of month. Which was true but when I woke up this morning, I regretted not making him at least pull out early. If I get pregnant, no way Rory would want me to abort it. He's liberal about everything but abortion. He thinks it's murder. How can it be murder when you're killing something the size of an olive? But he goes berserk on the subject because his mother almost aborted him. She even went to the clinic, but it was a week too late.

Working all day with a hangover was a nightmare. And not a word from Dan. Why does he let that crazy bitch answer his cell phone anyway? God, I wish I hadn't called. Someone shoot me in the head. Pretty please?

Thursday, November 15, 2007

I pour my heart out but all notme58 wants to know is how Rory's band got its name. Well, notyou, the story goes like this. The three founding members each wrote down five words on five separate scraps of paper and put them all in a hat and pulled out three at random. The words came out in exactly that order. Fascinating, huh? It's an awesome name, isn't it? Although I think Assassin Epiphany Cream would have been even better. But fate decided it.

You guys, please stop accusing Glenn Warburg of wanting to bone me. It's so sad that every time a man spends more than ten minutes talking with a hot girl everybody assumes it's sexual. Ever heard of platonic? Or maybe he likes women his own age. Or maybe Glenn's into guys. I don't know and you sure don't either. So shut the fuck up.

. . .

Thanks to all of you who wrote to tell me my number of discrete visitors is completely phenomenal. I had a feeling it was. Yay! I'm finally good at something!

Madmantype said the only reason I'm getting so many views is because I sound hot and I let Dan have oral sex with me. Hey, whatever it takes to get ahead. That was a joke. Get it? LOL!

Friday, November 16, 2007

I just called my dad and asked if we could have lunch tomorrow, just the two of us. This is code for "leave your pathetic Indian girlfriend at home." He said yes but I could tell he was annoyed. He hates being alone with me. I don't know why. He didn't used to. Up until junior high we did things together all the time. Maybe it's because now that I am older I often want to discuss money. The subject is unbearable for him because it reminds him of what a deadbeat dad he is.

Let me explain. When my parents got divorced the judge ordered my dad to pay $1,600 a month in child support. That was almost eleven years ago which means by now he should have paid us a fortune. You do the math. Well, guess what? He's paid a total of $300! Which was the amount of the check he wrote my mom in the courthouse hallway three minutes after the divorce papers were signed! He asked her to be patient about getting the rest, because he'd just handed in a story to a magazine and there was going to be a delay. Well, the delay lasted forever. Great guy, huh? Today he's too sick from drinking to even work, so he lives off Social Security checks and his hardworking Indian girlfriend. He also gets occasional handouts from his rich aunt Dorothea in Florida.

What irks the shit out of me is that my mom doesn't really care that he's a deadbeat dad. I think she actually sort of likes it. It makes her feel even more superior to him. She loves to say that after she kicked him out she never took a red cent from him. But she never needed to! She's the director of human resources for a big insurance company and makes awesome money and benefits. I, on the other hand, am broke off my ass. My life would be so much better if I had just a small percentage of the money he owes us. I could buy a car, for instance.

What's really sad is that even though my dad is poor, he could get me a car so easily. All he'd have to do is call up Dorothea and tell her it's an emergency, because I can't function without one. She'd make him eat a little shit first but she would definitely write a check.

Still no call from Dan. Maybe French Fry never told him about the hang-up call. How lucky would that be?

I got paid today. 32 hours x $12 an hour = $384.00 cold hard cash.

. . .

If my dad complains tomorrow about us eating at a restaurant, I'll tell him to relax. It's on me. Ha!

Saturday, November 17, 2007

Yesterday when I called my dad he was so drunk he forgot that the Michigan–Ohio State football game was on today. So instead of us going out to eat we stayed in and watched TV as usual. Which means I dressed up for nothing.

My father is completely in love with sports. I'm sorry but I think a semi-racist middle-aged white man wasting a whole day in front of the tube, watching a bunch of poor black kids chase a ball around a field is just plain pathetic. And it's even worse that he does it wearing dirty pajamas, with a belly as big as a pregnant lady's. Last year Jade's older sister Mylene, who's a telephone triage nurse, told me it's not fat that makes my dad's gut so huge. It's his liver. She said "Go to your computer and look up cirrhosis." I did. It was horribly sad. He is also diabetic now too. He has to shoot up every single day.

Unlike baseball, when football is on I'm only allowed to talk during the commercials, so I had to tell my dad about my new job in two-minute chunks. He didn't say much back. He hardly talks these days. He is very sick. He is so skinny he can barely lift his beer mug with his skeleton arm. He hasn't cut his white beard and white hair in ages. He looks like he's 100 but he's only 54. He is definitely going to die pretty soon.

When he does talk it's usually to crack a lame joke. For example, when I told him I work at Elysium Books, he said "It's all Greek to me." When I said World War One was called "the war to end all wars," he said "Too bad Hitler never got the memo." And when I told him Glenn was paying me 12 bucks an hour he said "Does that include hand release?" I used to think it was cool I had a dad who makes sex jokes. Now I just think it's inappropriate and tragic.

The whole time I was there, his Indian girlfriend Affie (her real name is Aafreen) walked in and out of the kitchen with trays of appetizers, smiling like one of those happy robot moms from the old sitcoms, only she's chubby, wears a sari and has a mustache. (Both my parents are dating people with mustaches. Only Mark doesn't wear a sari. He is sorry. Ha!) I don't know where Affie comes up with these recipes of hers. She served us weird crabmeat in little pita breads, squares of stinky cheese toothpicked to sweet pickles, egg-salad sushi rolls and macadamia nuts covered in bacon and curry.

While she's feeding us this garbage, my dad's insulting her right to her face and she doesn't even care. He told her that her crabmeat tasted like cat puke. I asked "When's the last time you had cat puke?" He said "The last time Affie made tuna fish." Ha! Later he said "I never thought I'd eat a pig in a blanket worse than the one I met in that Mexican whorehouse in 1974." Later he said "It's not that Affie's a bad cook. It's just that she's not used to cooking with American ingredients. We use shrimp. They use crickets." Affie smirks at these insults like he's some naughty boy instead of a grown man who basically hates her guts.

Another terrible thing about hanging out at my dad's is that he keeps all his windows closed even in summer, so his apartment, which is very small, reeks of cigarette smoke, incense and cat poop. Affie owns a stray named Tapu that is dying of leukemia. It must be invisible or the biggest coward of all time because even though it is an indoor cat I have never seen it once. The place is so stinky it makes me want to run out the door screaming and never come back. But you're not allowed to do that, right? Honor thy parents.

Sometimes during the game, he looks over at me and I can tell he's thinking something. Or feeling something. Something important. But I have no idea what. The only way I know he loves me is that every now and then I will hear him on the phone and he'll say "Can't talk. My gorgeous daughter is here," or "Gotta go, the fruit of my loins and I are enjoying some quality time."

You'd think maybe at halftime we might have some sort of conversation but not even then. He just sits there sipping beer, watching the marching band or the highlights like it's the most suspenseful thriller he's ever seen. Like it's *The Wages of Fear* and any second a truck is going to blow up. I usually don't care—I'm used to it—but today he knew I had something I wanted to talk to him about. I was so pissed he wasn't even curious what it was that I asked for a cigarette and a beer. I usually hate being self-destructive in front of him because it sets a terrible example, but today it was either that or stick my head in the garbage disposal.

Affie ran to get me a beer like it was the most exciting thing she'd ever done. My dad handed me one of his Kent Lights. Lately they are my brand too. They taste like car exhaust and burn as fast as fuses but I think this will eventually help me quit. I held in the first drag for about ten seconds. Ahhh! I felt so much better.

When the game was over, I said "Can we please talk? Or is this a doubleheader?"

"I know that tone," he replied with a cruel smile.

"Huh, I wonder why. She only raised me. Yes or no? Otherwise I'm leaving."

He was pissed for a second, then he looked at Affie. "Baby, how about giving me and my spawn a little privacy?"

Even though her feelings were hurt, Affie smiled all the way through the hanging wooden beads into the bedroom.

"Okay, lay it on me," he said.

I told him how scary it is to defer college, and how I'm still not sure what I want to do with my life, and how hard it's been for me with all my friends away at school, because I depend on them for transportation, and most nights I just sit home lonely because I have no way of getting anywhere. My dad knew what was coming.

He said "So tell the bitch to buy you a car."

My mom is always the bitch, the witch, the ballbuster, the shrew, the hag or the cunt. Why you ask? Why does he speak of her with such offensive disrespect? Because he's still in love with her! Even Affie knows it and she doesn't know much.

I replied "I've asked her a million times but she thinks I'm too much like you. She thinks I'm an alcoholic. She's worried I'll die in a fiery crash."

This was total bullshit. My mom has no idea how much I drink. If she did, she'd ground me forever. The real reason she won't buy me a car is that she thinks I am lazy. My 2.75 GPA makes her sick. She knows what I am capable of. But if I told my dad this, he would be off the hook.

"Neither of those accidents were my fault," he growled.

"I know that, Daddy. But she thinks they were. She thinks they were caused by your excessive drinking."

"Sanctimonious hag. If she had her way, we'd all be drinking holy water."

"Out of the pope's nutsack."

This really cracked him up. He totally forgot that it's his own line that he's said at least three times. Boy, does he love it when I bash my mom. He was all buttered up now. I scooted over on my knees and squeezed his bony hand. The fingernails were yellowish brown from smoking and he smelled of Old Spice and B.O.

"Daddy, my whole life you said you'd buy me a car when I turn eighteen. Well, I'm almost eighteen. Please keep your promise. Please!"

He looked at me with a gooey little smile.

"What about your rock star boyfriend? Freckle Face. Why can't he squire you around?"

"We broke up."

"Oh, too bad."

"No, it's not. He's been pressuring me to . . . you know . . . go all the way. I'm not ready."

Boy, did he love that! What dad wouldn't? Hahaha!

He smiled even gooier. "Eighteen and still a virgin. I must have done something right."

We both smiled at his miraculous achievement. Our eyes met. It was one of those moments that is really warm for like half a second then turns instantly uncomfortable. He reached for another cigarette. His hand shook.

"You know, when you were little, you promised me you'd never grow up. You said you'd stay my little angel forever. But you lied. I mean, look at you now. Tits and everything."

When he saw how shocked I was, he looked really embarrassed. He covered it up with a smile and lit his cigarette. His dead eyes returned to the TV. He blew smoke and took a big gulp of beer. Then he wiped his mouth with his pajama sleeve and said that at tax time he'd look over his finances and get back to me about the car. In other words "Go home."

Monday, November 19, 2007

I told Glenn Warburg today about how when it was time for me to start kindergarten, I was held back because I was born in December. So instead of going to school, I stayed home and my black nanny Ethel taught me how to read. When I finally started kindergarten I was already such an awesome reader that after just a few months they skipped me to first grade. When I got the good news, I ran to all my friends on the playground and sang "Kindergarten baby, stick your head in gravy, wash it out with bubble gum and send it to the navy!" My mother loves to tell this story. She thinks it's hilarious what a disloyal little bitch I was.

I also told Glenn how I continued to love reading all the way until my eleventh birthday when against my mother's wishes, my grandma bought me my first computer. A lime iBook. Pretty soon I was spending all my free time emailing friends and wasting time on various websites. If there was a word I didn't know instead of looking it up in the dictionary I went to answers.com, and if I was assigned a book report, instead of actually reading the book I'd use SparkNotes. I'm pretty typical of my generation, I told him, only I never got into computer games, and pop music means nothing to me.

I said that when I want to relax I watch classic films. Preferably foreign or in black and white.

"Such a shame you stopped reading," Glenn said leaning back in his squeaky wooden chair with his hands behind his head. His sweet blue eyes got sort of misty as he talked for ten minutes straight about how he couldn't imagine his life without books. "Online stuff is fun," he said, "and so is TV. But all they do is make you feel closer to everyday life. The same with most movies. Great literature does the exact opposite."

"Makes life less fun?" I asked.

"No, no, it lifts you out of the here and now and brings you closer to the angels."

"You're religious?" I asked, pretty surprised.

"Not those angels," he said, smiling at me like I was a cretin but cute. "I'm speaking metaphorically. I'm talking about transcendence. Escaping the daily and the ordinary. Leaving mortality behind."

I told him about a kid from my class named Alan Hsia who got perfect SAT scores and is now at MIT. He told me once that when he plays the cello he leaves his body and disappears into a world where he has no problems. I was blown away by this because he's fish-faced and zitty and unless he turns out to be gay I am pretty sure he'll never get laid in his entire life, so for his problems to disappear is a huge deal.

"Is that what you're talking about?" I asked.

"Yes. It doesn't have to be literature. It can be a musical instrument. Or a great painting, a great opera or ballet, even great love. All of them can give you a feeling of transcendence. So can religion. You leave the earth behind. Death means nothing. You're alive in the eternal present."

"Can great TV do it?"

"No. Magazines can't either. Or fashion. Or pop music. Nor anything on the Internet."

"How do you know? Are you sure?"

"Yes, because they're all evanescent. They appear then disappear in a mist. And we really wouldn't want them to be any different. That's their particular charm."

I wasn't sure I understood anymore.

"Now don't get me wrong," Glenn said. "These things are all wonderful. As I said, life would be much less fun without them. But fun cannot compete with transcendence. No way, no how."

In the afternoon I had nothing to do for an hour. Instead of doing whatever online, I roamed the stacks. Glenn said I can borrow any book I want as long as it isn't a first edition. I found a book with an amazing title: *Who Was Changed and Who Was Dead* by Barbara Cummings. I've only read 13 pages so far but it's absolutely wonderful. It starts after a big flood. Swollen dead farm animals are floating around in the living room of an English house. Very biblical. The hero is a girl whose cruel father makes her hate all men. I would have read more but I kept stopping to daydream about how cool it would be if I were an intellectual like Dan or Glenn and knew at least a little bit about pretty much everything. I don't think Dan would have forgotten me so easily if I was a girl like that.

Wednesday, November 21, 2007

Just so you all have something to be thankful for tomorrow, I am going to allow you to get to know me better by filling in stupid questionnaires.

Q. Are you single?

A. Almost never.

Q. What is your favorite number?

A. 69 and sometimes 96.

Q. Are you happy with your life right now?

A. No, ask me again in two minutes.

Q. Are you committed to your boyfriend/girlfriend?

A. Help, I can't breathe! Someone take the pillow off my face!

Q. What is your favorite subject in school?

A. Me. Also out of school.

Q. Do you love to shop?

A. Only till I drop. Then I like to sleep.

Q. Do you have cash?

A. Yes, ask me again in two minutes.

Q. Are you an extrovert?

A. If you mean a slut, the answer is yes.

Q. Have you ever had sex with someone of your own gender?

A. Only once. Tasted like Chicken. Of the Sea. Ha!

Q. What would you rather be doing right now?

A. Resting my head on Dan's manly chest.

Q. Can you blow a bubble?

A. Yes, anything.

Q. I dream about _____.

A. When I will fall in love. Really in love.

Q. I worry about _____.

A. My dad dying before he buys me a car.

Q. I wonder how come _____.

A. Tastes on the rocks. Ha!

Q. Do you like Bush?

A. No, home wax.

Q. Do you like roller coasters?

A. I live on one.

Q. Does your family do fun things together?

A. Only when I was little.

Q. Does sex mean love?

A. No, but love definitely means sex.

Q. Last baby you held?

A. Never.

Q. Last text message you received and from who?

A. "See you tomorrow, beeeaaatch! Turkey Day! Hell yeaaaah!"
From Jade.

Thanksgiving, November 22, 2007

I didn't even know how much I missed Jade until this morning when I heard a car door slam and I hurried to the window and there she was, running across the lawn waving and screaming at me. We met downstairs in the middle of the staircase and gave each other the biggest hug in history. We were so close this year that a lot of kids at school seriously thought we were lesbians. At senior prom, just to make their lives more exciting, we tongue-kissed in the middle of the dance floor. Just long enough for the cheerleaders to scream and their boyfriends to pop boners.

Since Jade's mom is Filipino and could care less about Thanksgiving, Jade was free to celebrate the holiday with us. (Jade's dad is a rich Iranian who lives in California.) This was perfect because at the last minute Rory's mother, who has M.S., guilted him into flying home to East Wakefield, New Hampshire, which meant we had an open place.

Since dinner wasn't until 3:00, Jade and I immediately escaped. Jade's car is an ancient vomit-green Honda with corduroy seats and only a cassette player but, hey, who's complaining? It felt so good to have wheels again! Jade used her fake I.D. to buy us some wine coolers, a pack of American Spirits and one of those freaky freezing-cold tuna fish sandwiches that I wouldn't eat even if I was starving to death in Darfour. We drove over to the high school and hung out on the empty practice field. It felt wonderful to be there and not have homework to worry about. There were autumn leaves on all the trees.

I won't bore you with the dirty details of Jade's trip to Manila but she had a blast with her second cousins and fell madly in love with a cute American boy one year younger than her. His dad's in the banking business and they had tons of hot sex. Not with the father, with the son. Ha! Jade always falls in love when she goes on vacation. She also falls in love when she goes to the mall. Or the movies. Or the dentist. She's pretty much in love with love. The sad part is, if the guy falls in love back, she dumps him superfast, but if he doesn't fall in love and just uses her for sex, she hangs on until he gets bored and dumps her. This can take months sometimes because she is absolutely gorgeous. Half Filipino and half Persian. A "flippin' A-rab" I call her, which she thinks is hysterical but her mother hates it, because Persians are not Arabs and she doesn't want the government to show up and waterboard her.

Physically Jade is my exact opposite. Five feet tall, 93 pounds. Awesome brown skin. Shiny, short black hair. Perfect teeth. Rock-hard butt. Tight legs from two years of running track. A little brown statue. I'd kill to look like that. Her only flaw is that a boy I know who boned her said she smells funny down there. Not horrible, just different. Foreign. I didn't like the sound of that! One Americano please! Anyway, the typical thing is, Jade says she would kill to look exactly like me. She says "I want them long legs, girl! I want that black-girl's ass!" (She calls my butt a "thing of booty.") In other words, the grass is always so much greener.

When it was my turn to talk, I didn't really have any hot stories to tell, except about Dan and the box job, but I couldn't tell it to Jade. She thinks all Dan and I have ever done is kiss a few times and that we stopped seeing each other back in October. She has no idea about Martine either. I am not sure what Jade would say if she knew the truth, but I do know that she is a terrible gossip and would definitely tell people. Dan is 32 and a professor. Me touching his dick is very big deal. What if the story got back to Rory? What if Jade told her mom? (Kids love to tell their parents horrible stories about their friends' behavior so that their parents will be grateful they aren't worse.) If Jade told her mom, her mom would definitely call my mom, and my mom would definitely call Dan's college and get him fired. She doesn't care if I have protected sex with a committed boyfriend, but an illegal affair with an older man would make her livid.

In the end all I told Jade about was my sex with Rory. To make it more exciting I pretended that I'm scared I'm pregnant and that it's the worst nightmare I've ever endured. I said I had already decided to "make like NASA and abort the emission."

When I moved on to the subject of my new job, poor Jade tried so hard not to look bored. But she was practically falling asleep. She is the least intellectual girl on earth. I doubt she's ever read an entire book in her life except maybe *Goodnight Moon* when she was three. As far as films are concerned, unless it's an incredibly raunchy comedy or an action movie, forget it. She's worse than Rory. Sometimes people ask me what on earth I see in her, and I tell them that I love her because she's an expert on having fun. She knows how to live. It's true. She doesn't worry all the time like I do.

After a while we had to pee. We did it behind an equipment shed on a pile of dirty rubber bases. While we were squatting I said "What if all the boys from school who had mad crushes on us drove by and saw us right now?" Jade laughed so hard she sprayed her new Nikes. I love that she thinks I'm hilarious. It makes me even funnier. ☺

After we got back to my house, I watched TV and Jade answered emails. It was hard for me to concentrate because Jade is very loud. A human calamity. Her laptop blared angry rap music and beeped with constant alerts, and while she was yelling at friends through her speakerphone, text messages came in like every two seconds. My mom walked by at one point and said "It's like a disco in here! How can you even hear yourselves think?" Jade laughed but the second my mom was gone she made a face and gave her the finger.

When it was getting close to turkey time, Jade jumped into the shower. This gave me a chance to check my email. Every single email I received today (except for spam) was from you guys. I officially have no more real friends! Just virtual ones. According to my tracking site 756 discrete visitors visited my blog yesterday. Yeehaw! I don't really care why it's happening, I just know I dig it. I am used to being famous only in my own mind.

One of you named munciemama22 sent me a video link with the subject line "Check it out!" Like an idiot I clicked without looking. It was one of those scary undercover videos from the anti-meat terrorists. I should have closed it right up but it was like in a horror movie when the scalpel's about to go into the eyeball and you know you should look away but you can't. Maybe that's not you. But it's totally me. I'm a glutton for punishment. But this video was way worse than a fake punctured eyeball. It was actual turkeys being slaughtered.

APPETITE SPOILER ALERT!!!

They grab the birds by the feet and throw them onto these moving stirrup things that catch them and carry them upside down to a machine that cuts their throats. Then they're dropped into a pot of boiling water to melt their feathers off. If the workers who did this were actual human beings with hearts maybe it wouldn't be so horrible but in the grainy movie I watched, you can hear the workers making sick jokes and bashing the turkeys against the machinery just for the fun of it. Also one of them pretends to fuck one of the turkeys. It's like what the soldiers did to those poor prisoners at Abu Graihb. Why do men need to fake-fuck everything? Men and women are supposed to be the same species but it's very hard for me to imagine a female soldier pretending to bone a helpless victim. She might stick her thumb up and grin at the camera to prove she is badass but that's all.

Although I'm not a huge meat eater, I do love me some turkey at Thanksgiving. Thanks a lot, munciemama22! Now every Thanksgiving for the rest of my life I'm going to have to push away memories of your heinous video! Or else eat tofurkey. Aaagh! Jade watched some of it too, and even though she screamed in all the right places, she wasn't as upset as I was. "Just block it out," she said. Easier said than done, right? Well, not for her. She had three huge helpings of dark meat. I could barely get down one slice of breast. Of all the images in the movie the one that freaked me out the most was of a bird that fought back so hard the blade missed its throat and it fell into the scalding water alive.

At dinner Jade and I drank sparkling apple cider and totally behaved ourselves, till Mark Aubichon suggested we go around the table and say what we were thankful for. It was hard not to laugh right there. I was fine when Mark bragged about his great job at a "high integrity" law firm and his perfect health and wonderful family and friends, but when he turned to my mom and said "Who would have thought that at the advanced age of fifty-six, I would meet a fabulous, smart, sexy lady like Diane?" I snorted cider out my nose and couldn't stop laughing. Neither could Jade. We didn't stop laughing for so long that it hurt my mom's feelings. But come on! Sexy? My mother is about as sexy as Hillary Clinton. Pretty face but cursed with cankle and tharm. Plus she wears bright jazzy dresses that look like they were made out of 1980s shower curtains.

My mom was so hurt by our rudeness that she let us leave the table early. Jade went to get wasted with some of her hardcore druggie friends by the lake. I stayed home and wrote this post. When she called a few minutes ago she asked what I was doing. I was dying to tell her. But I couldn't. Without my anonymity I am dead meat. I am turkey. Gobble, gobble, gobble. Hahaha!

Friday, November 23, 2007

The subject of slaughtered turkeys has got me thinking that people have two choices in life: Live with your eyes open or live with them closed. If you live with them open you see reality as it really is. If you live with them closed you only see your fantasies. (The film *Vanilla Sky*, as well as the Spanish film it was based on, deals with this concept.) Well, I hate to admit it but I live in fantasy like most people. I hardly ever seriously think about AIDS or global warming or all the bloody madness happening in the Middle East right now, and until the turkey video I'd never really thought about how animals are slaughtered. If I did keep my eyes open and let in reality, I honestly don't know how I would ever get out of bed and live my life. How could anybody?

How do you go to work and laugh with your friends if you know that at that exact second your government is dropping a huge bomb on an Arab's house that turns out not to have any terrorists inside, just families?

When I occasionally do open my eyes and face reality (like when I watched the turkey video) I feel terrible about the world and wish I could make it better, but everything I can think of doing seems pointless. Political stuff seems the most pointless because there's so much lying and corruption. The only thing that might make a difference would be some gigantic violent act against an evil corporation, but even if I was dying of cancer I don't think I would have the guts to do it.

These are the kinds of dark thoughts I've had since learning how turkeys die. This is why I choose fantasy. Maybe that's why my dad became a drunk. Because he had the same dark thoughts and drinking made them disappear.

Saturday, November 24, 2007
I am sorry. I should have explained. Cankle = calf ankle. Tharm = thigh arm.

I am too high right now to right about anything other than being high.

Sunday, November 25, 2007

Jade is the worst influence. Way too drunk. Just hurdled. Hahah! I mean hurled.

Monday, November 26, 2007

You won't even believe what I'm about to tell you. Sit down and light up a joint or fix yourself a nice double scotch because this is serious. (It's so sad and awful that I am still in denial about it.) This morning I was in the kitchen eating cereal and reading the newspaper, which I almost never do. Ironically I was reading an article about how less and less people read these days. Like 40% of American adults didn't read a single book last year! Anyway, I started thinking about Glenn and what he told me about the transcendence of reading, and I decided to write down the name of the article so he could read it online, in case he doesn't get the paper delivered. As I stood up to get a pen I saw my mom standing in the doorway staring at me like a crazy owl. Something was truly wrong.

"Sweetie, come with me," she said.

My first thought was that my dad was dead.

I said "What is it? Just tell me!"

Her face stayed serious and she reached out a hand. I let her lead me down the hall to her office. Mark Aubichon was waiting there at her computer, which was weird because he never sleeps over on a school night, which means he must have come over superearly.

My mom spoke first. "We're really sorry to have to tell you this but—"

"When did he die?"

"What? Who?"

"Dad isn't dead?"

"No, no!"

Mark wiggled a finger for me to come closer. On the screen a website showed a big map of our town with about 20 little red triangles all over it. Mark pointed at the triangles and said "Each one of these represents a registered sex offender." He clicked on a red triangle about two blocks from downtown and up came an old police mug shot of Glenn A. Warburg. That's right, my boss, but looking much younger and meaner. He was wearing a green and yellow camouflage T-shirt. He had zits and a buzz cut. Underneath the pic it said:

Conviction(s)
CRIMINAL SEXUAL ASSAULT
Source of Information: State Offender Registry

I was in shock.

Mark said "I'm sorry, kid. I know you were really excited about this job but that starting salary of yours just didn't pass the smell test with me, so I decided to poke around and see if I could learn more about him. Never did I expect to find something like this."

"Glenn's a rapist? Is that what it means?"

"Sexual assault is a broader category than rape. The particulars can vary, but yeah, it's basically sexual contact without consent."

"Against the woman's will," my mom said really slowly like I was a mongoloid.

"Or the man's will," Mark said. "We have no way of knowing the victim's gender. Although it wasn't a minor or else the charge would indicate that."

"You have to quit your job right now," my mom said, walking over with the phone.

"What do I say?" I asked.

Mark laid a hairy-knuckled hand on my shoulder. "Just tell him your mom's boyfriend got you a job in his law office. Which by the way is the truth. There's an opening in the copy room. It doesn't pay twelve bucks an hour but—"

"No, thanks."

"Are you sure?"

"I'm way too original to copy."

They both laughed which was what I wanted because it gave me a chance to escape.

"I'll call Glenn from my room," I said.

Glenn is such an outstanding human being that it took me a half hour of sitting on my bed squirming and biting my fingernails before I could get myself to pick up the phone and call. When he answered I did the best acting I could, telling him about my wonderful new job in the copy room of Mark's law firm of high integrity and how impressive this would look on my resume if I decided to become a lawyer. Remember when I said the worst thing in the world would be a boss who can tell when you're lying? Cancel that. It's a rapist boss who can tell! I was pretty sure Glenn knew I was bullshitting but what could I do? If I told him what I had found out about him, he might lose his shit, come over and criminally sexually assault me.

I'll never know whether he knew I was lying or not because all he said was how sorry he was to lose me and what a wonderful, special girl I am and how much he'd miss me. I said I'd miss him too. He made me swear to drop by next time I was in the area. You bet I will, buddy. Cross my heart and hope to get raped. Ha!

I wish I could have an honest conversation with Glenn A. Warburg about his crime. I am dying to know what he did and why he did it and who the victim was. I am positive it was a young girl, I don't know why. I crave every single detail. I love crime shows. I remember once a long time ago I was driving my mom crazy with questions about something, and she said "Oh god, I've given birth to a journalist!" And her boyfriend at the time said "No, a cop." How funny is that? Me, a cop!

. . .

Since I no longer have a job, I didn't know what to do today, so I spent the entire day doing nothing.

Phone ringing. Stand by. Someone loves me.

Jade. She feels so bad about me losing my job she wants to take me out drinking tonight. I said yes. It's unhealthy to spend an entire day indoors.

Friday, November 30, 2007

Many of you wrote to me furious that I didn't blog once this week. Well, here's why: I hate blogs about nothing. I don't care about how messy your sister's room is or how much you paid for your new figure skates or what that bitch C.C. said to you at the bar mitzvah that hurt your feelings. I assume you feel the same way. Isn't life boring enough without me adding to it?

What if instead of taking the week off, I had told you the truth about my life? How I was so depressed about losing my job that I slept all day and watched as much bad TV as possible? How I lived on rice cakes, beer and little boxes of raisins, and pretended my pillow was Dan's chest? How I only went out looking for work once and after an hour I had to pee so I gave up.

Oh, I almost forgot to tell you about my nights! Monday

I drank with Jade, Tuesday I smoked with Rory, Wednesday I drank with Jade again, and last night I drank and smoked with Rory. I have the worst bags under my eyes. Oh, yeah, and Tuesday night I had sex with Rory on the floor of my room. He came even faster than usual because it had been a while. Afterwards we went out to *Beaowolf*—a highly unimpressive film. We shared a large buttered popcorn. Is this really the sort of meaningless crap you want me to blog about? Yeah, I didn't think so.

I have been chaining all week. So bad that at night when I am trying to fall asleep, I hear a little whistle in my lungs that scares the shit out of me. Women die from lung cancer like ten times more often than men. I would love to quit smoking right now but I know if I even see a beer bottle, I'll start again. To quit smoking I need to quit drinking, and to quit drinking I would have to stop being depressed, and to stop being depressed I would need something good to happen, or even have the hope of something good happening.

Saturday, December 1, 2007

Around 7:00 tonight my landline rang. When I answered it a man said "Katherine?" and my first thought was that I must be in deep shit, because I never use Katherine except on official documents.

"Yes?"

"Paul Spooner. I don't know if you remember me."

I said I did not.

"I interviewed you for college."

"Oh, right!"

It was easy to remember him because I applied to six colleges but only showed up for one interview. I had no choice but to go to that one because my mom's uncle went there and left them a shitload of money when he died. If I hadn't shown up, it would have created a family scandal. My mom said I was pretty much guaranteed to get in and she was right. Honestly? With my grades and scores there is no way in hell I would have gotten in without help. I won't tell you the name of the school but trust me it is excellent.

I took a cab to the interview which was in the fanciest part of town. An area of beautiful homes, tall trees, and boring rich people. If I hadn't gotten baked the night before the interview, I would probably remember it much better now. I know Mr. Spooner is some sort of stockbroker, with a really sweet, sensitive face, curly black hair and a muscular body. And I remember what I wore. I dressed Hepburn-sexy. Katherine not Audrey. Conservative but cute. Knee-high riding boots from Spain, a tailored shirt, a skirt with just enough leg showing and a long tweed coat. It was perfect. Except for my hat. I wore a purple ski cap because a lying bitch at school told me that purple was the school's color. It's not. Not even close.

I remember in Mr. Spooner's living room there was a framed photo of him and his wife. She and I looked sort of alike. Her skin was better than mine because she's not a teenager, but I have bigger boobs, a skinnier body and a cuter nose. I liked that there was a resemblance because it meant I was his type and that he would probably like me. I don't remember exactly what we talked about but I remember we laughed our asses off and he was totally non-judgmental. I didn't bullshit him at all. I told him about my drunk dad and even about my three days in the psych ward and he was interested and sympathetic.

One thing he said that day stuck in my mind because it was extremely cool. He said when he was a teenager back in the '70s he and his friends used to smoke a ton of weed. His mother knew about it and she used to laugh at them and say "Marijuana helps adults relax after a long hard day. What the hell do you kids have to be anxious about?" Mr. Spooner said he felt pretty silly when she said that but now that he is an adult he realizes how wrong she was. It's teenagers who need dope the most because nothing compares to the hell of being a kid. A grown-up who gets how hard it is to be a teenager! ☺

Anyway back to my story. When Mr. Spooner called me tonight he said: "First of all, congratulations. You were one of only three students I interviewed who got in."

"Wow."

"Second, I saw your name recently on a list of kids who took deferments. Is that right?"

"Yeah," I replied. "I felt like I needed a year to figure out what I wanted to do with my life. That way I could get the most of college when I go."

"Sensible."

"My mom thinks I'm insane."

"So what are you doing with yourself? Do you have a job?"

"I did. At a bookstore. But I had to quit. I found out the owner's a registered sex offender."

"You're kidding."

"Nope."

"Jesus, that's terrible."

"Even worse for the girl he raped."

He laughed. It came back to me how much I liked him at the interview. I started getting that fluttery butterflies in the heart feeling you get when a boy in fifth grade calls you at home for the first time. Which, if you think about it for like a second, is a pretty weird way for a girl my age to react to a man old enough to be her father. But, hey, I never claimed to be normal!

"Look, Katherine—"

"Katie."

"Katie, I don't know if you've ever done any babysitting

but my wife and I just lost our nanny. She moved back to Guatemala to take care of her dying sister and left us high and dry for the holidays."

"That sucks."

"It sucks even worse for her dying sister."

My turn to laugh.

"How would you like to be our full-time nanny for a few weeks? From eight to four every weekday until Christmas. I remember you said how much you love kids."

This totally confused me because I don't love kids at all. I panicked and wondered if maybe he was mixing me up with someone else.

"You'd work through Christmas. Then we go on vacation for a week. In the new year, if you like the job and we like the job you're doing, we could make it a permanent thing. If it's not working out on either side, we part ways with no hard feelings, and at least you helped us get through the holidays and you picked up some extra cash."

"You live pretty far away. I don't have a car. Is that a problem?"

"We've got an extra one. A Volvo. But here's something you should know. Our son Cole's only fourteen weeks old."

"Wow. I've never really taken care of a tiny baby before."

"If you're up for it, my wife Maggie'll teach you. It's easier than you think. He sleeps half the day."

"I'm up for it."

"Fantastic. It pays thirteen bucks an hour. If we need you to stay late, it goes to fifteen."

I said very casually that it all sounded fine. Meanwhile I was overjoyed, jumping up and down like a maniac. Right then Rory walked into my room and thought I'd finally lost it. I signaled for him to shut up. As soon as the call ended, I ran right past him down the hall to my mom's room. She was as happy as I was and really proud of me for making such a good impression that Mr. Spooner would trust me with his baby.

I wanted to go out and celebrate immediately of course, but Rory had to be up with his band at the crack of dawn to travel to a gig 12 hours away. All week he's been asking me to come with him but no way am I going to be trapped in a farty van with a bunch of guys listening to loud music and playing computer games. Anyway now that I had a new job starting Monday it was a mute point because I needed to be fresh and rested. So instead of celebrating we talked till I yawned my brains out and he got the hint. As soon as he was gone, I called Jade.

"Bitch, get over here right now! 'Cause I gots to celebrate!"

Just my luck she met some cute boy at the Gap this morning and they had plans to smoke hash. I was so desperate I called Merci Gregoris, my smiley, fat, bleached blonde, mole-covered lab partner from high school who goes to the same college as Rory. She answered on the first ring but she was in a car full of sorority twats. I was the last person she wanted to talk to. Highly ironic when you consider that in high school she would have had a heart attack if I had ever asked her to do something on a Saturday night.

Friendless, I poured some wine, lit a cigarette and called my dad to tell him that my boss turned out to be a rapist but that I already had a wonderful new job. He didn't give a shit until I mentioned that it came with the use of a car. Boy, did he perk up. He's off the hook now. Asshole.

I am too excited to sleep. I wish Dan was here. I am going to call him and tell him that I have a car now and that any time he wants I will come over and make love to him. That's what I want. Sex with him just once. Then I will fall asleep on his safe chest, and in the morning before we part forever I will tell him how I truly feel, even though I know he doesn't feel the same way about me. I am going to call right now. If Martine answers, so what?

LATER: 1:23 a.m.
I did it! I called Dan! He picked up on the first ring. I could tell by the way he whispered that Martine was pretty close by. Maybe even in the same room. He knew all about my earlier hang-up call but wasn't that mad, although he reminded me of our deal.

"I call you, remember? I call you."

"But you never do!" I said really shaky, like I was about to start crying.

This melted his heart a little.

"Yeah, I know. I'm sorry. I've been busy. So what is it, sweetheart? What's going on?"

"Nothing really. I just miss you and I wanted you to know that I got a great new job today and it comes with the use of a car. Which means if you ever want to me to come over to watch a film, I can. I want to. Any night. Any time. Just tell me when. I'll be there."

I said it in a soft intense sexual way. It definitely worked. His breathing changed. He was remembering our last night together. How hot it was. How I touched him. Boner rising! Hahaha! When he finally talked, his voice was full of manly desire.

"When do you get the car?"

"Monday morning."

More heavy breathing.

I could hear him flipping through his calendar.

"Friday night. Come over at seven."

Even though I was disappointed that it was so far in the future, I said perfect and he gave me the directions.

It's 1:47 and guess what? Now that Dan has invited me over I'm not that psyched about our date. I'm actually pretty sad and scared about it, to tell you the truth. Crazy, I know. But he's way too old for me and it's a shitty thing to do to Rory. I'm not respecting him or myself. So why don't I just cancel the date? Because I can't. I lack will power.

Why am I still awake? I need to look cute for work on Monday. Sleep, gyrl. Ha! I doubt it.

Monday, December 3, 2007

The first day of my new job is over. It is only eight o'clock but I am going to go to sleep now. Why? So I can wake up and do it all over again tomorrow. Yipppeee. If I owned a handgun I would definitely shoot myself right now. No lie. Babies are the worst things ever invented.

Tuesday, December 4, 2007

I have purchased a handgun but I am too tired to load it. Just kidding. Babies are screaming poop machines.

Friday, December 7, 2007

Okay, so I didn't post for three days. What's the big deal? Hey, I've got an idea. How about you guys GET A LIFE! I am working hard to get one and if I succeed, guess what? I will quit blogging immediately. Why? Because people with lives don't blog. They don't even read blogs. Didn't you know that? LOL! It's true!

Can you tell I am dangerously caffeinated?

Where do I begin? Mr. Spooner's wife's full name is Margaret Elizabeth Whitley-Spooner. If that isn't a Waspy name I don't know what is. She looks like a wider-hipped and wider-shouldered version of myself. When I say that she is wider please don't think she's fat. She's just, as my dad would say, "broad of beam." He would probably also say "I don't know whether to hand her my cock or a field hockey stick." Or his favorite advice which is "Never screw a girl who can beat you in an arm wrestle." In other words, she is athletic but not fat. Although she is not cute and sexy (like me!), she is definitely beautiful. You could shave her head and add 30 pounds to her butt and she would still look awesome. Fabulous bone structure and smile. The kind of woman a rich guy marries if he's smart because she'll never cheat on him or spend too much of his money, and she'll make his house look like it's out of a magazine.

I love my mom but she is the exact opposite of Margaret Spooner in every way. For example, the inside of our home is painted like a pre-school. Our living room walls are red, white and yellow. My mom calls it playful. I call it butt-fugly. The Spooners' house on the other hand is truly elegant. The walls are white, the floors are dark wood and the furniture is antique. The bright comfortable kind not the dusty stiff kind that looks like it will break in two. Before having a baby, Margaret was an interior decorator and it shows. That's how she and Paul met. He hired her to decorate his bachelor pad.

Margaret and my mother are opposites about food too. Except for special occasions when she actually cooks, my mom is a microwaver. Her favorite foods have dangerously high fat contents and are loaded with white flour. Things like pizza pockets and four-cheese macaroni and cheese. Margaret is a health nut who thinks microwaves cause cancer (or maybe it's sterility) so she cooks everything from scratch with organic ingredients. Fiber is her life. Her food is not only delicious but amazing to look at.

Even though I blogged that I hate being a nanny, I take it all back. Margaret is the greatest boss ever. The reason I was suicidal those first few days is because I'm not used to waking up early. Or taking orders. Every single second of the day Margaret was telling me what to do and how to do it, and it was freaking me out. I had to learn how to swaddle, shush, burp, change a pissy diaper, change a poopy one, clean gums and give a bath. (Don't forget the butt crack and uncircumcised wiener!) Margaret is one of those mothers who has read every single baby book in the world and wants to do everything perfectly. Even if she gets no sleep she doesn't care, because she will do whatever is best for her baby. With so much to learn and being so tired all the time, of course I was grumpy. By the time I got home I couldn't even go out for a cocktail because I was dead on my feet. I don't know how Margaret does it.

Tuesday night after I blogged, I had a nightmare that I accidentally left Cole in the bathtub and he drowned. I woke up shaking and crying. I looked around in the freezing dark. It was almost morning. The alarm clock was just about to go off. Another day of work already! This was my low point. I wanted to run down the hall and flop onto my mommy's stomach and tell her to call Margaret and say I had spinal meningitis.

Thank god I didn't because Wednesday everything changed. I started to have fun. I think it's because girlfriend started to acquire some skills. I swaddle and shush great now, almost as well as Margaret, and I'm not scared of getting Cole in and out of his little plastic tub. I am also very good at getting him to sleep. Maybe because I sing better than Margaret. (She is tone deaf.) You won't believe this but I love changing poopy diapers now. If you've never changed a baby's diaper you will think this is freaky but baby poo smells wonderful. I huff it like glue. They should make a perfume out of it. Newpoop by L'Oreal. I'm serious. Margaret says it's only true of breastfed babies. She says the poo of bottle-fed babies smells like shit. Hahaha!

It's pretty obvious I'm excited to see Dan tonight.

. . .

What else can I say about Margaret Elizabeth Whitley-Spooner? Oh, yeah. She gives me brakes all day. Whenever Cole is napping or feeding I can do whatever I want. Some nannies have to tidy up and do the laundry but the Spooners have a Jordanian housekeeper named Aziza who comes three mornings a week for four hours. Margaret says she refuses to hire a Mexican, because as warm and friendly as they are, they are not meticulous. She says it's "alien to their culture." I don't think she is being racist when she says this, just honest. At lunchtime I can either go out or eat in, taking whatever healthy food I want from the humongous fridge. Even though Margaret despises smoking, she gave me my own personal sterling silver ashtray to use on the patio. I think it's impressive that she doesn't let her own dislike of the habit get in her way of being a good hostess.

What else about my job? Oh, yes, Paul. I saw him a little bit on Monday and he was very nice, but then he left to go to San Francisco all week on business. He didn't return home until this morning. He is not a stockbroker as I thought. He manages some sort of fund. He must be very good at it, because he is filthy rich. Margaret is sad that he travels so much. I also think she gets insecure that she is home changing diapers all the time while he is out in the world meeting exciting, beautiful women. I don't blame her. I am sure there are a lot of sneaky bitches out there who would love to steal Paul away from her. Even though she is so good at being a mother and loves Cole to death, I know she misses being a fancy decorator.

She shows her insecurities in the form of jokes. Once she called herself "a boring housewife" and another time "a fat zombie." She also said "Don't make Cole love you too much or I might get jealous." And then once while I was swaddling Cole she said "You're getting so good at this, Paul's going to hire you to replace me!" And then this afternoon when I walked to the door after Paul paid me she whispered "Remember when my ass looked like that?" Paul did not reply which I thought was the smartest choice.

It's time for me to jump in the shower and drive to Dan's. I will blog every single dirty detail. I promise. Wish me luck!

xoxoxo[3].

Katie Kampenfelt

Saturday, December 8, 2007

Driving home from Dan's last night I tried to figure out why things are suddenly so much better between us. Is it because distance makes the heart grow fonder? Or is it because I have a car now which makes me seem more independent and exciting? Or is it because in one week I will be legal? (For sex with older guys, not for alcohol.) Whatever it is, we weren't older guy and younger girl last night. We were just equals.

Let me start at the beginning. Where else? Ha!

I dressed extra cute: dark green corduroys, red rubber boots, a white shirt, a red wool reindeer-pattern sweater, a white ski jacket, and green mittens. It was perfect because Christmas lights are up all over the place and I embodied the holiday spirit. When I got to his street I didn't even need to read the house numbers because I could tell which of the cheesy new town houses was his by the massive book and DVD collection in the front window.

When he opened the door he looked so different I was shocked. He has a beard now. No, not a bushy ugly one, thank god. A short one with sexy gray in it.

I said "Look at you!"

"What about me?"

"The beard."

"Oh, right. I always grow one when I'm working too hard. You like it?"

"Uh-huh."

"Good. Come in."

He was wearing a black cashmere sweater over a white T-shirt and his usual faded jeans. No shoes. His socks were thick gray. He looked strong and broad-shouldered.

I get so used to being with Rory who is cute, skinny and practically pubeless that it's easy to forget what a real man looks like. I was carrying a bottle of red wine that I stole from my mom. Dan took it out of my hands and quickly shut the door behind me. He was scared the neighbors would see!

Except for being bigger, the new place looks a lot like the old one. There is only a little new furniture. Some of it is more modern than I would expect him to like.

He smiled at my holiday outfit and said "You're awfully festive."

"You like it?"

"Are you kidding? You're an adorable snow elf."

"Christmas is my favorite holiday."

"You could make a Muslim convert."

"That's my goal."

Usually we don't kiss until at least a half hour after I get there and I always make the first move, but not this time. He reached out and took both ends of my scarf and pulled me until our lips touched. Then he kept kissing me all the way to the couch. We fell down on it. Man, did he miss me! It was crazy hot! "Major grindage," as Rory would say, and then he started ripping my clothes off until all I was wearing were my socks and he was performing his oral specialty. I didn't explode but I got as close as I've ever gotten with another person in the room.

Afterwards he was lying there breathing hard with his cheek resting on my hip bone. He was smiling up at me all proud because he thought he had succeeded. No way was I going to tell him the truth. Whenever I tell guys I only cum when I am alone in the bathtub with my trusty shower hose, they go crazy wanting to be my first. But the harder they work at it the more I think and the more I think the more impossible it is for it to happen.

I really wanted to give Dan another box job but I didn't want it to seem like I was doing it just because I felt obligated. Anyway I didn't even have to decide, because Dad jumped up and handed me my clothes. All I put back on was my T-shirt. Not even my underwear. Usually I'm pretty modest once we stop fooling around but I thought it would be fun hanging out like this. I was right. I felt grown up, sexy and European.

This would normally be the time when we would raid the fridge for junk food and he would start hinting that it was time for me to go. Not last night! Instead he called a restaurant and ordered lasagna and Greek salad, lit some candles and opened the wine I brought. I was sort of in shock but I didn't say anything. We ate on the counter in his brand-new kitchen. Everything was so clean it was almost scary, like eating in a chem lab. He told me how insane and depressing everything has been with Martine lately. He said that one night she screamed at him so loud he came close to hitting her. The next day he passed his neighbor on the way to the car and was too embarrassed to even look at him.

"You ought to dump her," I said very casually, chewing a garlic ball like it didn't matter to me one way or the other.

He said he would love to except that once before they met she tried to kill herself by cutting her wrists the wrong way and he was scared she might try it again. He said he could not live with the guilt. I understood that. The good thing about Rory is that when I dump him, no way he'll kill himself. He'll just kill me. Hahaha!

Later Dan said that the one thing he has learned from his mostly terrible relationships is "never to try to save anyone." He said every single one of his girlfriends was "a wounded bird." He said trying to fix their broken wings was futile. First of all it hardly ever works, so most of the time you end up stuck with this needy, depressed, one-winged person, who you eventually dump, which makes you feel incredibly guilty. But on the tiny chance that it does work and the person starts to become less insane and damaged, then they hate you for knowing them when they were a disaster. They can't wait to fly away on their two working wings and find a new boyfriend who has no clue what a mess they were before. Either way you end up alone and unhappy. Dan says he knows Martine's never going to get better and that it's just a matter of time before he dumps her, but he would like to find a gentle, kind way to do it so that she doesn't reach for a razor blade again.

"You really think she'd do that?" I asked. "You're positive she's that into you?"

He laughed. "I guess I could be wrong. Maybe I'm just flattering myself. Maybe she'd move on like I never existed. Man, would that be sweet."

Back on the couch, finishing off the bottle of wine, I told him some details about me and Rory. I used my favorite line, how the thing I love most about Rory is that he loves me. How I'm not in love with him at all but that I'm afraid to dump him because I'm scared of being alone. How since I was 11 years old, I have had a boyfriend every single minute except for about three months.

"So you're just staying with him to satisfy your own self-ish needs?"

"You got it, pal."

"I guess we're both narcissists then."

"No way! I hate my stomach way too much!"

"Shut up. You have a beautiful body."

I pinched my pooch and told him I was going to get lipo-suction.

He howled with laughter.

"It's as tight as a snare drum!"

He's wrong.

We discussed narcissism for a long time. He said it doesn't mean being in love with yourself, the way most people think. He said that Narcissus in Greek mythology was in love with his own reflection in a pool of water. An image of himself. Which is different. In other words narcissists fall in love with how they think the world sees them. I didn't really get it, so Dan used me and Rory as an example. He said I go out with Rory because I like seeing myself the way he sees me. I use him like a pond of water or a big living mirror. Rory's idea of me feeds my starving ego. If I truly loved myself I wouldn't need him for this.

Normally I would have been offended, because what he said was pretty insulting, but I could tell he wasn't judging me. How could he? He suffers from the same condition. I told him he was right. I basically only see Rory when I feel like shit because I know he'll tell me how beautiful and sexy I am. And in bed what turns me on is not that he's a good lover. It's that he gets so turned on! I love that my body drives him insane. I feel like a porn star or something. My bad mood goes away.

"But not for very long, right?"

"Maybe an hour."

"There you go."

We smiled at each other.

This was the first time we'd ever had a really serious conversation about our lives. Usually he just teaches me about film and I ask insightful questions. I crawled over and kissed him. When it started to get hot again, he got scared and pushed me onto my side. We spooned for a while not talking.

Finally I said, pretty much to myself, not really expecting an answer "I wonder why my self-esteem is so shitty."

"Considering your relationship with your dad, it would be a miracle if it weren't."

I rolled over and looked him in the eye, because this was important. "There's something I've never told you. Besides being a stingy asshole, my dad's also the world's worst alcoholic. He has cirrhosis. He's going to die from it soon and he's only fifty-four."

What a stare he gave me.

I laughed and said "I know what that look means. It means you're going to tell me to stop drinking again."

He didn't deny it. I pretended to slap him. He caught my hand and kissed my fingers. Then we made out some more. Then he tucked a piece of my hair behind my ear. The way he gazed at me you'd swear he was madly in love.

"If I'd met you when I was in college," he said, "I would have worshiped you just like Rory does. I would have been a jealous maniac too."

"You mean you don't worship me now?"

"I cherish you. It's different."

"Better?"

"Much. The thing about being put on a pedestal is you take one step and you fall face-first in the mud."

God, I love brains.

Compared to Dan, Rory is a full-fledged dunce.

After we washed the dishes, Dan filled the bong and put on a French film called *The Grand Highway*. It was absolutely enchanting. Every action in the movie, even the simplest things like fishing, meant so much more than the obvious. (The symbol for Jesus Christ is the fish.) But then as usual the pot kicked in and the whole room started spinning. I thought "What the hell, I might never see him again." So I crawled off the couch, knelt down, unbuttoned his jeans and gave him the longest, most amazing blow job in the history of French cinema. He laid there afterwards smiling at the ceiling and said "This might be the greatest date ever."

Yay! I agree!

When I got home, my mom and Mark Aubichon had just gotten back from a party. They looked at me funny, probably because of my beard-burned face and stoned happy eyes. I ran upstairs, laughing. Mark thinks I'm a slut but I don't give a shit. Hahaha!

I've wasted half the day writing this. Why? Because I promised you I would and I'm a slut who keeps her word. My weekend's half over. What shall I do tonight? Know what I want to do? Nothing. Yup, you heard me. Just lie in bed and dream about last night, playing it over and over again in my head. A gyrl is only happy to stay home alone on a Saturday night when she's truly in love.

My PMS will be starting any second now. So unfair. I'm sick of being sad. I want to stay smiling forever.

Sunday, December 9, 2007

Last night after I blogged, instead of doing nothing, Jade and Rory convinced me to go out. Normally I would never hang out with them together. They hate each other's guts. But last night they were both so desperate to see me I made an exception. Jade needed to see me because she dumped her new boyfriend. Turns out he has herpes and didn't tell her until after about the 20th time they boned without a condom. Oops! Sorry! And Rory needed to see me because his balls were deep, deep blue. He'd never say that, of course. He says he misses my pretty face.

I made sure I drove so that if they started fighting I could escape. I warned them both that if they didn't play nice I'd strand them on the side of the road like red-haired foster kids. Ha! To balance things out Rory invited Willy Schmidt to come with. He's the only one of Rory's roommates I like and the only one who's not in the band. He's stocky but kind of soft like he's never worked out a day in his life. He has a big smile and a blondish Afro and wears football jerseys with his jeans. (It's forgivable because he wants to be a sports agent someday.) Willy is one of the sweetest, smartest, funniest guys you'll ever meet, and if I wasn't so superficial I'd marry him.

We went to a movie called *Awake* which Jade heard was amazing. When it was over, Rory and Jade were so busy drooling over Jessica Alba's ass they didn't bother to mention that the movie was dreadful. The epitome of everything Dan and I despise about Hollywood. Thank god Willy agreed with me or I would have had to drive all of us into a tree. Next time I see Dan I will give him my vicious review. He jokes that he counts on me to keep him current on pop culture. He says I save him a fortune in movie tickets.

Rory wanted to go to this cool new strip club where he knows the bouncer, but Jade's mom was out on one of her rare dates, so we decided to take advantage and hang out at her big tacky house instead. Jade's dad moved out when Jade was in about the fifth grade. He had a sick love of mirrors and marble. You have never seen so much of both. The house looks like a giant bathroom. You can't even eat at their dining room table because the whole time you're seeing nine of yourself.

We got extremely high in the den which is still filled with her dad's gold-painted furniture and books in Persian. Almost as soon as we turned on the TV, Jade and Willy got lost so Rory could maul me. We boned right there on the leather couch which stuck to my ass and made weird farting sounds whenever he pumped. It made me laugh, which pissed Rory off, because he said if I were really into it I would not even hear the sound. Oops, sorry. Guess I'm not that into it then.

Jade didn't inform me of this until later, but while Rory and I were in the den, she and Willy were in the kitchen. She leaned back against the fridge, grabbed his head, tongue-kissed him then pushed him down to his knees. And he did it! He lifted her denim skirt and ate her like a poodle! With all the lights on. And mirrors everywhere. The last thing I would want to look at during sex is a hundred copies of my own bright thighs.

"But you don't even like him!" I said.

Jade replied "I don't need to like a guy to let him give me head. I can even hate him. Just as long as he knows what he's doing."

Her eyes looked shiny and evil for a second. It really kind of scared me. But maybe I just imagined it because I feel so protective about Willy.

So that was my night. I should have just stayed home, right? Why is it so hard to stay home on a Saturday night? Why do we always think something exciting and new is going to happen when it never does?

A psycho opened fire today at a church in Colorado, killing four people before a security guard shot him dead. I've seen many news stories like this before, but watching this

one I cried like a little bitch. Why? Because I am a deep
person? Because my heart is full of compassion? Because
I love my fellow man? For a second I thought it was all
three. Then I realized it was none of the above. Hormones,
baby!

I just called my dad to inform him that my big birthday is
less than a week away. Since he is off the hook about the
car, I'm hoping maybe he'll be so relieved he'll give me
something really good. He wasn't home. I left a hinting
message.

Wendola95 wrote to me, laughing her ass off that when I
was describing my big date with Dan, I wrote "Dad" instead
of "Dan." Thank you so much. If you were not 13 years old
I would hunt you down and kick your teeny-weeny ass.

Monday, December 10, 2007
Friday night was too wonderful for words. I cannot stop
thinking about Dan. So guess what I've decided? When I
tell you, you're going to suggest I return to the psych ward
for a big cup of pills. I want Dan to be my boyfriend. Yeah,
yeah, yeah, I know it's caaa-razy but it's not like we have to
get married. We can just make each other happy for a while,
and then when it's time for me to go to college or for him to
get married, we'll break up and stay friends. And if we can't

do it, if it's too painful to break up then maybe we're one of those one in a million couples where age doesn't matter. Like Charlie Chaplin and his wife Una who were way farther apart in age than us but got married anyway and had many children. They were still together years later when he died at the age of like 99. She was still pretty gorgeous and he looked like a miniature mummy in a wheelchair. I know this because before we watched *City Lights* Dan told me all about their love affair and showed me pictures of them online. It was my first silent movie and I really loved what I saw of it. Dan shouldn't have told me about the Chaplins if he didn't want me to get ideas!

To make it easier for Dan I will be very grown up and cool about certain things. For example, I won't force him to introduce me to his friends, family and co-workers. Obviously if he wants to that would be flattering and wonderful but if he doesn't, that's fine. Another thing is I won't get needy if he's busy writing his P.H.D. and we don't speak for a few days. I will live my life and trust that he loves me. Third, I won't turn into a French psychotic before my period. I might cry for no reason and eat a two-pound bag of candy corn but I won't call him a "selfish pig" and throw lamps at his head like Martine does. And the best part of all? I will let him have sex with my hot young body whenever he wants to. How great is that? How lucky is he?

Tuesday, December 11, 2007

Margaret and I took Cole to a particular kind of baby class today called Rye. Paul is really into it. Rye believes in respecting babies and letting them do whatever they want just so long as they don't hurt themselves or others. In class we laid Cole down on this big soft mat and then we were instructed to sit against the wall and observe as Cole interacted with all the other babies. Margaret was only allowed to butt in if Cole really needed her emotionally. He didn't. Not much happened really. Only 2 of the 8 babies were even strong enough to turn over. The rest just laid there looking at the ceiling. They cried a lot. Sometimes they reached over for the only toys they were given—cloth napkins and the lids of plastic food containers. I wanted to cry too. I could not stop thinking about Dan. When will he call? It better be soon. Is he afraid of me now because I gave him a blow job? So many guys do this. Things get really hot sexually and instead of being psyched about it they start to disappear. It's like they think you automatically want to marry them.

Many of you are really pissed at me for not answering your emails. Why should I? All you do is rag on me, call me names and correct my spelling, punctuation and grammar. You think I'm going to defend myself to you? Neeeevvvver!

. . .

Only Airesinmo said something positive. She thinks my relationship with Dan is thrilling and romantic. She finds guys under 25 as dreary as I do. She wishes she had a brilliant sexy older man like Dan to love and learn from. Hang in there, gyrl. You'll find one. Just wear short skirts and don't be afraid to make the first move. Older men are weak! Love you tons.

In four days I am no longer jailbait. My mom offered to buy me an iPod with fancy speakers. I told her I would prefer cold hard cash.

The best part of my job is every day at 3:00 when Paul comes home from work. He calls it "Happy Hour" not only because he has a G&T to relax but because we are all so happy to see him. We hang out and laugh and talk and he kisses the baby every ten seconds. What a marvelous father. It's like a big celebration!

Wednesday, December 12, 2007
My obsession interfered with my job performance today. I was carrying Cole in his basket while daydreaming about Dan. All of the sudden the basket shifted and I came really close to dropping Cole onto the tile floor. Scared the shit out of me! I stood there for like 10 seconds, clutching the

basket, while my heart pounded. Can you imagine if I had cracked their baby's skull open on the kitchen floor? People forget how scary it is to be a nanny.

I needed to do something to stop being obsessed, so after work I drove straight over to Jade's. When I walked into her mostly pink bedroom, she was downloading all the new music she missed while she was away.

"Yo, get off the computer, dude. I need your help."

"Fuck you."

"In your dreams, dyke."

This is how we speak to each other. Some people find it disturbing, others think it is hilarious. My idea was for Jade to call Dan for me. If I called and Martine answered, that would be way too risky. Two hang-ups in one week? I don't think so. Sure I could say "Oops, wrong number" but then she would hear a young female voice and that might make her suspect something. Jade was the perfect solution because if Martine answered, Jade could say "Oops, wrong number" in Tagalog, the native language of the Philippines. It sounds like a combination of Japanese and throwing up. Jade isn't fluent but she definitely knows enough to fake a wrong number. Martine would be way too bewildered by the foreign tongue to get suspicious.

Unfortunately to ask Jade to do this I would have to tell her that I was still seeing Dan and that it had gotten way more serious. As you know, I love Jade to death but don't trust her at all. Why is it short girls always have such big mouths? But since she was so perfect for the job, I decided it was worth the risk. But first I made her swear on her vaginal health that she would never tell a single living soul what I was about to reveal. She got very excited. Nothing a blabbermouth loves more than a new secret not to keep!

I told her way more than I planned. Everything in fact. Here's the funny part about her reaction—Jade was not judgmental at all about me cheating on Rory or even that Dan was cheating on Martine. The only thing that freaked her out was the age difference. She said that when an older guy goes out with a teenage girl, he's either a letch who's just using her body as a sperm bank or he's emotionally retarded. I told her that for a slut she was being ridiculously neo-conservative. I told her Dan was not emotionally retarded at all, that he is a mature and complicated man. And as for the sex, if anyone was using anyone, it was me using him. He'd gone down on me about 12 times and I'd only gone down on him once.

I used Jade's landline for the call. That way if Martine pressed *69, all she'd get was Jade's mom's outgoing voice message which is very middle-aged. While the call was ringing I whispered to the ceiling "Please god let him answer. Please god let him answer. Please god let him answer."

Because there's no such thing as god, Martine answered on the third ring. Why does he let her answer his cell phone?! Is he really that whipped?!

I quickly handed off the phone and Jade yelled out something in Tagalog. I imagined Martine's snobby French face staring at the phone and saying "What the fuck?"

After Jade hung up, I laughed so hard I almost peed.

"What did you say to her?!" I asked.

" 'Where is that clock that we ate yesterday at the bathroom in the church?' "

I friggin' howled!

Wrong numbers often come in twos so I knew I had a gift certificate for one more call. We killed a minute watching *Project Runway* on TiVo. Or as Jade calls it, *Project Bunway*, because it's mostly freaked-out homos trying to sew on buttons before the time runs out. Jade said that pretty soon all we're going to have is reality TV because the writers who write real TV shows are on strike. I had no idea. I am an ignorant teenager who lives only for love. I've got to read yahoonews more often. I dialed Dan's number again and handed Jade the telephone. This time he answered. Smooth as silk, Jade said "Please hold for Miss Katherine."

I grabbed the phone and spoke superfast.

"Don't be mad! I just need to talk to you, okay? Call me back on my cell as soon as you can. If Martine asks you who it was, just say some chick spewed a foreign language at you. Bye!"

Hang up.

Mission accomplished.

High five!

Jade and I then ate a veggie pizza and a spinach salad and watched some more panicking homos. I pretended to be in a good mood but inside I was praying for the phone to ring. Every few minutes Jade would ask another question about Dan. She was fascinated by our relationship. It was like she had just found out that I boned a dolphin or something. "Does he kiss the same? Does his skin feel different? Does he smell funny? Do you ever run out of stuff to talk about? Do his balls sag?"

"Stop being such a close-minded American," I said, getting annoyed. "In Europe, girls date older guys all the time."

I told her about Charlie Chaplin and Una. Jade had never heard of either one of them. I told her that maybe if she dated older men she would know who Charlie Chaplin was and wouldn't be such a judgmental whore. She laughed at this. One of Jade's best qualities is her ability to laugh at her own many faults.

Driving home through the frosty night with my ass toasting in the leather seat, I started to get scared. What if Dan was furious at me for calling? What if he never spoke to me again? My heart started racing and I was sure I was going to crash. Then my phone rang. When I saw it was Dan, I screeched over to the side of the road. I picked up and before he could yell at me I said "I'm sorry, I'm sorry, I'm sorry!"

"Relax. She ran out for cigarettes. She'll be back in five minutes. What's up?"

He didn't sound mad at all.

"I need to talk to you about something."

"Yeah, I figured. What?"

"Nothing bad, I promise. But I need to say it in person." I made my voice all soft and sexy. "When can I come over?"

His breathing stopped.

I whispered like I was excited but scared too. "What I did to you last time? I want to do it again. Other stuff too. Everything."

He didn't talk but I could hear him start to breathe again. Slow, heavy and full of passionate desire. He was remembering what happened last time. How amazing it was.

Finally he answered. "Friday at 6:30."

"Perfect."

I hung up fast.

Ha!

I am so going to burn in hell!

Friday is going to be epic. Please send me your votes. Should I ask him to dump his girlfriend and go out with me before or after we make love? If I ask him before, he might say yes because he wants to make love to me so bad. If I ask him afterwards, he might say yes because he wants more of what he just got. Is this confusing? Tough.

Must sleep now. I have a baby to take care of.

Phone ringing. Somebody loves me. Stand by.

LATER: 1:28 a.m.

Rory and I just had the hugest fight. He recorded a new song inspired by our relationship called "Blue Balls in Blue Jeans" and he wanted my honest opinion. He sang it for me over the phone. I told him I thought the tune was extremely catchy and cute but that the lyrics were juvenile. Since he wrote the words and not the music he went completely insane. I cannot love Rory because I cannot respect him. He doesn't take life seriously. If he did he wouldn't write silly songs like that. Older men rule. ☺

Thursday, December 13, 2007

I got basically no sleep last night but it didn't matter. I was so happy about my upcoming date with Dan that I couldn't stop smiling all day. My heart felt big and bursting with love. I wanted to hug the whole world. Even ugly old ladies and dirty old parking meters. I especially loved the Spooners.

For no reason Margaret gave me a Mexican silver ring she never wears and a gorgeous old Hermes scarf. Paul made a shitload of money today on some foreign deal so he brought home champagne and Belgian chocolates and we all indulged. He started fake-dancing Margaret around the room. It was the most in love I have ever seen them and it made me smile till it hurt. For the first time it felt like Christmas was just around the corner.

Friday, December 14, 2007

Monday we're going to the pediatrician to get vaccinations for Cole. Some parents don't like to give them because they think they cause autism. Paul decided that he'd rather give Cole his shots and have some small chance of giving him autism than have him die of polio or whooping cough that could have been prevented.

Cole has big intelligent blue eyes. Margaret calls them "vigilant." Which means alert and watchful. And his lips are pouty and full, the kind movie stars pay big money to get once they are at the age when nobody wants to kiss them anymore. Ha!

While Cole was napping I went to yahoonews to learn more about world events. I read about a teenage girl in Canada I think, or maybe England, who's in critical condition in the hospital after being choked by her own father for refusing to wear a Muslim scarf around her head. And I thought my dad sucked! Even if my father was strong enough to kill me with his bare hands, he would never do it. Unless I stole his last beer. As much as I want to know more about the world, it takes a lot of courage to read the news. I complained about it to Paul and he said not to worry my pretty head over it, because the world has always been shit. I felt better.

As soon as I got home, I started to get depressed. Maybe I'm scared at what might happen with Dan tonight. Or maybe because tomorrow is my birthday and I will be an official adult. One good thing—at least my period is over. Must get into the shower and do some strategic shaving.

Welcome to my reality show.

Sunday, December 16, 2007

I turned 18 yesterday. Adult life has started and all I want to do is die. My worst birthday ever. Let me put it this way. It was so bad I had an urge to go to church this morning, okay? I haven't been since I was 12. I am an atheist but this weekend made me feel dirty and ugly. At least my mom's church is clean and beautiful.

. . .

My date with Dan started exactly like the last one. We kissed at the door and walked with our mouths connected all the way to the couch. He stripped my clothes off and everything was exactly the same except that after he was finished going down on me, instead of me just lying there thinking about what to do next, I pulled him up to my mouth, kissed him deeply, unbuttoned his jeans, grabbed his dick and put him inside me. He was so shocked he pulled out a little but I pushed him back in.

I've only slept with six guys and two of them were once and one of them was three times. Rory is by far the person I've had the most sex with and it never lasts for very long. The sex with Dan was so much better than anything I have ever experienced, I can't even tell you. First of all, it lasted 43 minutes. (The clock was right near me.) And second, it felt absolutely awesome. I don't know if it's because he moves better or because he's got a bigger dick or what but it felt totally different. It just kept building and building until there was nothing in the whole world but the two of us and what we were doing. When he was about to cum and moving really fast, it felt so good I screamed and he had to put his hand over my mouth so the neighbors wouldn't hear. He kept pumping but he forgot to remove his hand. I had to pull it away so I could breathe. A pretty unromantic way to end the best sex of your life but in a way it was a sign that everything was about to get really bad.

We laid there kissing and breathing until I felt some dribbling and excused myself. I walked slowly to the bathroom because I didn't want to leak on the floor and because I wanted him to get a good look at my ass. I read once in one of my mom's *Cosmo* magazines that a good trick is to hold an open hand across your ass like a fan and sort of skip all the way to the john, so the guy won't see your cellulite. Since I don't have any I walked slowly with no hand.

When I came out of the bathroom Dan had his jeans back on and looked really freaked out.

"I wish that hadn't happened," he said.

"You mean no condom? Don't worry. My period ended this morning."

"No, I meant—"

"Oh, you mean jail? Don't worry. I turn eighteen in a few hours. I'm basically legal."

"Sit down, Katie."

I hated the serious look on his face. It was the kind your mom gives you when she got a call from the principal's office about the beer they found in your locker. It was not the look you want from a person five minutes after you make love for the first time.

"Here's the thing. I like you, Katie. A lot but—"

I knew what he was about to say. My heart stopped. But I pretended to be really calm.

"Listen, before you dump me, let me just say something, okay?"

He was so shocked by my mature attitude that he let me talk. I told him I really loved him and that I thought he should dump Martine and make me his girlfriend. But in a healthy way that would work with our age difference. He wouldn't have to introduce me to a single person. Our relationship could be totally secret. Just the two of us in his house, enjoying sex and food and classic films. And then as soon as he met a non-psychotic woman he wanted to marry and have kids with or I was ready to start college, we could break up maturely and stay friends forever.

I could tell he was impressed by my offer and how confidently and clearly I explained it. I honestly think he might have said yes but then I made a big mistake. I mentioned, sort of half joking, the Chaplins and how if it turned out we were like them, one of those one in a million couples that have a big age difference but really belong together, that would be cool too. We could get married and have many kids. His whole face changed. He pretended to think some more but I knew he had made up his mind.

"Katie, I'm so tempted. You have no idea. But it just . . . It's impossible."

"Why?"

"I know I complain about Martine. A lot. But there's something I haven't told you. About her. And me. You see, we're . . . well . . . we're engaged."

"What?"

He nodded his head, really embarrassed.

"You're just saying that to get rid of me! No way you can marry her! She treats you like shit! She's insane!"

He couldn't even look at me. "Not all the time. Sometimes we're happy. Most of the time actually. When we are, I don't call you. So you don't hear about it."

I started crying. "What do you have with her that you don't have with me?"

"Oh, sweetheart. Let's not start that."

I went sort of berserk and shouted "Answer the fucking question!"

He looked at the front door like he thought any second the cops were going to come busting in and find out I was only 17. But they didn't so he took a deep breath and talked really calmly. He said a bunch of stuff about how individuals of the same age share things that people with an age difference can't. Something about cultural references and existentialist clocks. WTF? Never date a professor! Then he said something that really pissed me off. He said that he and Martine were "intellectually compatible" because they're both working on their P.H.D.s. That was a cruel thing to say, because at my age even if I read a book every single day for the rest of my life I could never catch up with her.

All I wanted to do was escape. I got dressed. He watched me. Say goodbye to my hot young body asshole! At the door

I turned around with tears in my eyes and said "How long have you been engaged?"

He looked at the blank TV. "Since October. That's why I moved. We needed more room."

"You mean she lives here too?"

"Yeah."

"Where is she now?"

"She has a seminar Friday nights. I'm sorry. I've behaved really dishonorably. I was weak. I couldn't resist you."

I shook my head like I pitied him and walked out. I crossed the street as slowly and confidently as I could just in case he was watching. When I unlocked my car door I looked over my shoulder. He wasn't watching. I felt like such a loser. A typical dumb teenager. I cried so hard driving home I almost crashed.

I wish this was the end of my tragic birthday story but it's not. When I got home Rory was in the living room playing Scrabble with my mom and Mark Aubichon. Since Rory was supposed to be at band practice tonight I used him as an excuse and told my mom we were having dinner together. Well, it turns out Alden, their drummer, broke his ankle this afternoon, so practice was canceled. Rory called to tell me but my phone was shut off, so he drove over to see if I wanted to go out. When my mom told him we were supposed to be having dinner together, he got really suspicious and decided to wait for me like a spider on a web.

When I walked in, my clothes and hair were messy and my face was red from crying and beard-burn. Since my mom is clueless about my personal life, she thought I'd been raped or something. So did Mark. They jumped up all worried but Rory knew better. He looked like he wanted to strangle me.

"I'm fine," I said, laughing and crying at the same time. "I saw a sad movie, that's all. God. Get a life!"

"Really? What movie? What's it called?" Rory asked.

I was totally busted. I ran up the stairs and he ran after me. The second we were in my room, he slammed the door. His eyes were crazy. This is when I usually scream "Nothing happened! You paranoid freak!" But instead I told him the whole truth. I said I was in love with someone else, an older guy, and that I just found out he's secretly engaged and that my heart was broken in a thousand pieces and I just wanted to be left alone. If you know guys, then you know exactly what Rory said next.

"Did you fuck him?"

I swear, a guy would rather have his girlfriend be in love with another guy she's never kissed than have a one-night stand with a guy she'll never see again. For a girl it's the exact opposite.

When I didn't answer, he covered his face and started moaning like I just got hit by a car right in front of him.

"Oh god, you did! You're a whore! A whore!"

"Yup, that's me."

He jumped and grabbed my shirt. I hardly blinked.

"How many times?!" he screamed.

"None of your business, you jealous ass! And it wasn't fucking! It was making love! Something you know nothing about!"

He pulled back a fist. No one's face gets redder than a red-haired person's when he's furious. I knew I was about to get my teeth bashed in, so I did the only thing I could; I punched him first. Right in the neck. He was so surprised that he fell and the back of his head cracked against my vanity. Before he could get up, Mark Aubichon rushed in, grabbed him by his hair and his arm and told him to get out or he'd call the cops. Now Mark was the one who looked deranged. A maniac frog. He shoved Rory out the door. Blood was running down Rory's head. I know I should have felt sorry for him but I didn't.

Later while I was washing my face, my mom came in and asked what was going on.

"Lovers' spat," I said. "The kind you and Mark would have if you were in love. Please get out."

There's nothing that hurts her feelings more than when she wants to talk about my life and I shut down. She stormed out, slamming the door behind her. The full-length mirror almost fell off. I crawled into bed with my clothes on.

I need a brake. My hands are sore from typing.

Later: 2:15 p.m.

On my birthday my mother and I have a tradition. We get a mani-pedi, eat a fancy lunch and see a movie, usually a chick flick. Yesterday I woke up so late we didn't even bother. We just sat in the kitchen and talked while I crunched down a bowl of Mark's natural cereal (pebbles and acorns) and drank a humongous mug of coffee. I felt so guilty about the way I spoke to her that I told her a lot. I left out Dan's true age, of course, and that he is an engaged professor but I told her pretty much everything else. I said that the night before, right after we made love for the first time, he confessed that he was getting back together with his ex-girlfriend and that he couldn't see me anymore.

"Oh, sweetheart," she said. "Never get attached to a boy if there's a third party involved. The third party always wins. Because they have shared history on their side."

"Now you tell me."

"If I had told you sooner, it wouldn't have mattered. Everyone has to learn these lessons for themselves, I think."

"Yeah."

My mom is pretty wise sometimes. But only with the lives of others. Before I went back up to my room, she gave me three hundred-dollar bills for my birthday.

. . .

I spent the rest of yesterday in bed, too devastated to do anything but watch TV. I didn't even pick up the phone when Jade called, which since it was my birthday was pretty shitty of me but I knew I'd end up telling her the whole disgusting story and I didn't want to relive it.

Around 5:00 she texted me that she had just heard from Willy that Rory and I broke up. She was coming over asap to take me out for a birthday dinner and cocktails so I'd better get my "filthy ass in the shower." She is so funny. It cheered me up. I got right in the shower and made myself look as pretty as I could. Not very.

At dinner Jade gave me a beaded pink leather case for my phone and a $50 gift certificate to Victoria's Secret. After a dinner of fried shrimp, salad and fries, the waiter brought me an apple pie a la mode with a candle in it. I wished for Dan to dump Martine. On the way out, two older men tried to pick us up but we rejected them with humor. We drove like forty minutes to this new bar that serves minors if they're gorgeous and female. We got hammered on vodka and cranberries. Was it enough to make me forget my pain? Yes and everything else.

When we were leaving the bar around midnight, a cute boy in a Santa hat said hello to me in the parking lot. I grabbed him by the fur on his parka and stuck my tongue down his throat so far I touched his lung. At least according to Jade. I don't remember any of it. Then I asked him if he wanted to "fingerbang me." She said he was so scared he ran away.

Okay, that was the single most boring post ever. I have become everything I hate.

Now it's freezing out, football is on the TV, I'm still hungover from last night and my fingers are stiff from typing this sad tale of a girl gone wrong. I am really unfortunate and empty. No boyfriend. No secret older man. No bliss. No college. Loser[2]

I should have broken up with Rory the second I met Dan. Or else been strong enough never to kiss Dan in the first place. One or the other. One or the other.

I really don't want to get back together with Rory. I am sick of his freckles and intense emotions. Plus his balls smell like vinegar.

Thank god my name is not really Katie and I am 100% invisible to the world or I would be so humiliated right now I would crawl into a hole and die.

My father totally forgot my birthday. Or maybe he just ignored it. I was his favorite person in the world when I was little. Now that I am grown up he hates me. Why? What did I do wrong?

I am a crazier gyrl than I thought.

Monday, December 17, 2007

Cole got a vaccination today and afterwards when he started to cry so did I. On the way home Margaret said she was really impressed that I had been so moved. She said most young people lack empathy. Especially beautiful young girls. It was wonderful to get a compliment like that so I didn't tell her that the real reason I cried was that there was a cheesy calendar on the wall in the doctor's office that showed two lovers holding hands on a perfect beach and it reminded me that I will never kiss Dan again.

Driving home I sat in back next to Cole. He was about as happy as I have ever seen him. He squeezed my finger and whenever I crossed my eyes at him or made a funny face he gently smiled. Wouldn't it be wonderful if we could forget pain as fast as babies do? But if we did, I wonder if we would learn anything. I mean, isn't it pain that teaches us life's most important lessons? I want to learn from the pain of Daniel.

. . .

When Paul got home from work we all hung out together in the kitchen. Margaret tossed a big salad and Paul popped pieces of cucumber in his mouth. Paul is brilliant and speaks with charm about every subject. I don't care at all about sports except when I'm faking it for my dad, but I understand it pretty well. Paul explained the steroid scandal, and I swear he made it sound exciting. He talked about how baseball, except for jazz and movies, is America's greatest contribution to the world's culture, and to see it dirtied this way really disgusted him. I hope Margaret knows how lucky she is to have a rich handsome husband who is never boring.

On my way to the car I turned around and looked at their big, gorgeous white house all lit up and twinkling in the cold, but so warm inside, and I thought this is what I want someday. And I can have it. All I have to do is make smarter choices.

Driving home I decided to cheer myself up by going on the biggest shopping spree ever. I bought two wool tops, three hoodies, two pairs of skinny jeans, two packs of hairbands, two lacy bras, two red undies, a pair of red ski gloves, a jar of all-natural anti-dark-eye-circle cream, five magazines, one makeup remover with cucumber and aloe, a phone charger for my car and a pretty black velvet dress with a bow in back which is the perfect combination of dressy and casual. Oh, yeah, and a pair of black patent-leather ballet flats. I spent my gift certificate from Jade, all of my mom's present and most of last week's salary but it only cheered me up a little.

When I got home and saw my bedroom, I cried for two hours. I am still such a little girl and I hated that it showed in my lavender and white bedroom. I threw stuffed animals around and broke a music box and wished I had never met Dan. My mind was filled with vengeful fantasies. I wished that I was pregnant so I could wheel our baby by his house and torture him. I wished I knew who the best man at his wedding was going to be so I could seduce him. I would take phone pics of his head between my legs and send them to Dan. And then I thought maybe I should seduce Martine instead. I love them seafood crepes! Ha! These nasty ideas did not make me feel better. I went downstairs and drank one of Mark's fancy Dutch beers. That helped. Then I came up here and drank two more beers and smoked about five more cigarettes and that helped some more. Maybe someday I'll be a famous alcoholic, chain-smoking writer. I'll write a book about me and Dan. I wouldn't have to make anything up because the truth is pretty fascinating. At least I think so.

. . .

I texted Jade three times just now. No answer. I bet that bitch is in love again just when I need her most. Probably with the kid in the Santa hat.

I got a birthday card today from Affie. A lame joke card. Only two days late. My dad didn't write anything inside, just signed it. The hopeless scrawl of a dying man. Usually I spend Christmas with them but this year they're driving downstate to visit Affie's mom. I'm glad they will be gone. They both suck.

Tuesday, December 18, 2007

I guess the babies got all the crying out of their systems last week because at today's RIE class (I misspelled it before) there was no crying at all. The babies just laid there on their backs checking each other out like shy kids at a party.

RIE doesn't believe in tummy time. Most parents put babies on their stomachs a lot, which mashes their faces into the floor or the mattress. They flail around pathetically. RIE believes "Why put a baby through that? Why make him unconfident like that?" They believe a baby will turn himself over when he's good and ready. I bet my mom gave me a ton of tummy time because even though I have an outgoing personality, deep down I am not confident at all. I can still taste the floor, if you know what I mean.

. . .

Being a great parent is such a massive effort. Margaret is tired all the time. Breastfeeding is really exhausting, she says. And since Cole sleeps in their bed at night, every time he wakes up even for a second he reaches for her boob and it wakes her up. The other day she said she feels like her brain is turning to oatmeal.

The idea of sharing a bed with my husband and my baby is very cozy and appealing but when do you have sex? Never, I bet. Paul must be under intense pressure down there. Ha!

After work I was so desperate for a sympathetic friend I called Merci Gregoris, my big-titted, fake blonde, moley ex–lab partner. She says a bunch of kids from our class are back for Christmas break and having a party. It's at the house of a computer genius named Freddy Black who wears bow ties every day. Maybe it will be fun. If not at least there'll be liquor. She's picking me up in 25 minutes. Must shower!

Later: 11:48 p.m.
I wanted to leave the second I walked into the party because the house was infested with techies. They will probably

make extremely nice billionaire husbands some day but right now they are shockingly awkward and neurotic. Plus now that they all go to Harvard and M.I.T., they are deeply up their own butts. Which is insane. If you are a scrawny male virgin with acne and greasy hair, the last thing you can afford to have is a superior attitude.

While I was getting a beer in the kitchen, a semi-cute kid named Anton Tuttle walked up. He's tall and skinny and designs computer games. He told me he's working on a game right now set during the Spanish Acquisition. (I have no idea what that is. It gets six million hits on google but on a variety of topics.) I tried to escape but he stepped right in front of me and said "We were in the same elective last year. Logic-Psychology with Mrs. Patterson. You don't remember me because you were too busy being the hottest girl in school."

"Yes," I replied, "being hottest truly is a distraction."

Whenever someone accuses you of something horrible, always admit it. People don't expect it. It makes it much harder for them to hate you. Anton laughed and asked what brought me to Freddy's party. I told him I had just broken up with two boyfriends on the same day and I was there to cheer myself up, but "so far so bad."

Even though this was a direct insult, he laughed again. He obviously gets off on being abused.

"Where you goin' to school?" he asked.

I told him about my academic limbo. He was impressed

that I had gotten into the school that took me but even more impressed that I had the guts to defer.

He said "I hear life after semesters is endless."

I told him that it is, which is why I work full-time and blog. I thought that this would impress him but he made a smirky face and said "What is it about chicks and blogs? They all have 'em."

What an arrogant ass.

"Not like mine," I replied. "I just started it, like, seven weeks ago and it already gets between 750 and 1,000 discrete visitors a day."

"Unless you've got a cam in your shower, no way."

"Oh, I do," I replied. "And another one in my toilet."

I didn't smile or even blink. He couldn't tell whether I was joking or not.

He pulled out a handy pen. "What's the URL?"

"Sorry, it's anonymous."

"Oh, I get it. You're scared for your friends to know about it because it's full of all the crap you tell your bestest friends over the phone only now you write it down for strangers to read instead."

"Get laid much? Or ever?" I said, crossing my arms and giving him the hairy eyeball.

"Come on, you know I'm right! It's totally self-indulgent, isn't it? All about shoes and diets. And boys, of course." Now he was really laughing. "Where's my soul mate? Why can't I meet him? Help!"

Normally I would never let a stranger hurt my feelings but my defenses were very low. I told him that everything he said was true. My blog was vomitous. I was a total cliché. When he saw I was about to cry he felt terrible. I was tempted to tell him the name of my blog just so he could see that I am a real person with a real life and that I hate trivia as much as he does. But I didn't do it, thank god.

As I was leaving, he gave me his email address and said in a warm voice that he'd had a crush on me since freshman year and he'd love it if we could hang out before he went back to school. That was very sweet. I instantly forgave him for his cynical rudeness.

Jade emailed me while I was out. Of course I was right. She is in love. His name is J.D. and he works as a DJ. How funny is that? I wonder if he's slysdexic. Ha! She says next time we hang out she'll tell me all about him. I won't hold my breath. There's no excuse for what a failure she's been as a friend.

Friday, December 21, 2007

I have tried all week not to sink into a giant depression, but it's really hard not to when you are all alone in the world and there are Christmas lights everywhere. The nights are so cold and black. This is why I haven't blogged. Too sad.

. . .

I have always had a boyfriend. My first was Jake Barsumian when I was 11. He put his hand up my shirt to rub my non-existent boobies and I was so embarrassed I stayed home from school for three straight days. Since then I have pretty much had a boyfriend nonstop. There's always a guy some-where waiting for me to get single. One of my exes said to me "You treat guys like cigarettes. You chain them."

I know I should be relieved that it's over with Rory. Now we are both free to find something better. But I still miss having someone to talk to every day. I can't help it. If I told this to Dan he would laugh and say "You miss him because you can't stand being alone with yourself. You miss his worship." He would be right.

Everyone is back for Christmas break but no one calls me.

Before I left today Paul asked if I wanted to work their annual Christmas Day party from 3:00 until 8:00. I would take care of Cole when he wasn't sleeping or nursing and the rest of the time I would just be a guest. The pay is time and a half, plus all the eggnog I can drink. Yum! I usually spend Christmas with my dad but this year he's out of town, so this is sort of perfect.

You should see the tree Margaret picked out. It's a noble pine which is more expensive than the other kinds but it leaves more room for ornaments. She looked so tired, I offered to stay late and help her decorate it but she said she has a very specific way of doing things that would drive me insane.

Paul paid me today—$624 because I worked overtime. I want to buy the Spooners a Christmas present but they already have everything.

Saturday, December 22, 2007

Please don't write to me if it's just to correct my grammar and spelling or to judge my actions. I am doing the best I can. By the way, I know how to use the word "whom." I just think that most of the time it sounds snobby and stupid.

Today I stopped thinking about myself long enough to buy Christmas presents. I bought my mom five books and two CDs off her Amazon wish list. I bought Mark Aubichon a fancy Scrabble set because ours is missing crucial letters. I bought the Spooners a gorgeous baby album to record every moment of Cole's blossoming life. And even though Jade is a barbarian bitch I bought her a dual outlet cigarette lighter for her car. Nothing for Rory or Dan. It's lonely not shopping for a guy.

. . .

Joel Seidler called me again to "grab a bite." In case you don't remember, he's my old geometry tutor. Big nose and wide hips. I never called him back because I didn't want to get Rory jealous. Now that Rory's history, I can call him. I need a friend. Especially a great listener like Joel.

Sunday, December 23, 2007

I actually laughed today. Really laughed. My dad called to remind me not to come over Christmas morning because he'll be out of town. I told him that I would have to be a world-class cretin to forget such an important thing and that I had already committed to working Christmas Day.

"For the rapist?"

"Yes, Daddy, I am going to let him bang me under the mistletoe."

"Well, then, you're what Santa would call a ho ho ho."

Not funny at all but he sure is fast.

I reminded him that I have a new job nannying. He pretended that he remembered.

"You're so lucky," I said. "What could be more fun than spending Christmas with an old Hindu lady?"

I just said this to get him going. My dad hates India more than any place on earth. I've heard him rant against it a million times but it still makes me howl with laughter. He hates their music, food, clothes, government, movies, accents, many-armed gods and that they are starving to death but

refuse to eat all those perfectly delicious cows. He says everything stinks in India. "Like Affie's cooking times a billion."
The whole country's nothing but a "curried mosh pit" with
open sewers that run right through cities like rivers, only
instead of carrying ships and tugboats, they carry "peanuts,
chickpeas, and corn." He says India's the most "awful, back-
ward, corrupt and beknighted nation on earth." He thinks
their cast system is cruel and he hopes that Pakistan nukes
India into a pile of smelly dust. What makes this whole
thing even more hilarious is that my dad has never been to
India! He's hardly been anywhere!

When Affie got home, he had to hang up fast. But it
wasn't because he didn't want her to overhear his racism.
She is never offended by anything he does or says. It was
because she just got back from the vet who put down her cat
Tapu because of its leukemia. Not even my dad is insensitive
enough to continue to insult a person's country while they're
crying their asses off. Especially when it's the person who
pays his bills and hands him his beers. I wish I could have
been there to see him comfort her. That would have been
funny. How do you comfort a person when your cirrhosis-
belly is so big you can't even hug them? Come to think of it,
how do you drive three hours downstate in that condition? I
hope he doesn't die at a rest stop. That would be tragic.

A born-again reader asked me how come I love Christmas so much when it's so obvious I am the worst Christian

in the world due to my sinful behavior and my "complete lack of remorse about it." Here are my opinions and feelings about religion. I think religion helps people get through life. When you think of how hard life is and how much harder it used to be, it makes perfect sense that people invented God. I'm not just talking about when we were in the caves being eaten by saber-tooth tigers but also not that long ago when babies died during childbirth and very often the mothers did too. If you did not believe in God back then I think you would go crazy with fear and sadness.

In my own pampered life I have found that I don't need religion so far. But that could change. There is so much about religion I sincerely love. Number one is Christmas, of course. I love everything about it, especially the myth of Jesus Christ's birth. Some people think that because it never really happened that makes it meaningless but I totally disagree. I think the fact that it's a myth makes it even more sacred and inspiring. How amazing that human beings would make up a manger, three kings, the shepherds, a virgin mother, a carpenter father. The humbleness and beauty of it!

Each day since Dan broke my heart, I am less and less angry. I mostly remember the good times now. His smell, his chest, his hands. It's starting to snow out. The wind off the lake is shaking my windows. I would give anything to be crawling into bed with him tonight. Or else outside, walking together in a winter wonderland.

Monday, December 24, 2007

My mother obeys the Catholic custom of cooking seafood on Christmas Eve. Tonight she served my favorite, linguini with lobster. Plus a big yummy salad with feta cheese, pine nuts and hearts of palms. Then we all sat around our fake Christmas tree sipping fancy apple liqueur and opening presents. My mom said that my gifts were thoughtful and terrific but that my real gift to her, as far as she was concerned, was how well I pretended our evening together was making me happy when it was obvious I was still heartbroken over the boy who had dumped me for his ex-girlfriend. Mark nodded with neckless sympathy and proposed a toast to the wonderful boy I was going to meet next who would treat me like royalty. Sweet, right? He means so well.

My mom gave me a bunch of presents but I won't bore you with what they were. The only good one was a three at a time movie subscription to Netflix. I will need this to continue my film education. Finally, I will get to see more than just the first 11 minutes of movies!

Very soon it will be Christmas. I should probably stop writing now or else I'll become one of those blogger-chicks

Anton Tuttle hates, the lonely kind who whines because they can't find their soul mates.

Maybe I will call Anton and have sex with him before he goes back to college. Boy, would that make him happy.

When I was little my mom used to force me to listen to an opera called *Amahl and the Night Visitors*. It tells the story of the night before Jesus was born. I would scream and fight and beg her not to make me listen. I would never tell her this but tonight when she played it before dinner, it gave me goosebumps and I came an inch away from sobbing. I will never be a little girl again and, man, is that sad.

Oh, yeah, it's "benighted," not "beknighted." Thanks for writing, Carmelo, and telling me what a benighted person I am. Merry Christmas to you too, douche bag.

11:59 and not a creature is stirring except my computer mouse.

Santa better not come down the chimney tonight because I'm so lonely I might blow him. Admit it, I am your favorite ho ho ho.

Have yourself a merry little, okay?

Tuesday, Christmas, 2007

Whenever peple ask me what my goal in life I always say tp figure out what my goal 8n life is. Now finally I know. To be Margret Sponer. I justgot back from the Spoonerss party (I am tooo drunk to type!!!) and I swear it was the most gorgeus ever. The house was amaz8ng decorated. The tree looked perfecwith antique ornaments and l8ttle lights. Could been a deparment store. Candles glistered everywhere. And the food looked more amazing to eat. uh-oh. What does that mean? Drunk! How Marg does 8t with no sleep blows my mind. Just to give you an idea there were little red bowls on all the en tables filled with chocolat coinswraped in gold foil. Well guess what? In the foil was printed "From the Spoooners!!!" Margaret printed it herself with some sort of litte mahc8ne. Now you know what I'm talkin' 'bout yo. The woman's a godddesss!

Now I shal hurl me down to sleep. I can't believe Paul let me drive hom this drunk. Unless maybe it d8dn't show. At the door Paul gave me week's payin cash for my Chrismas bonus." I am rich.

Wednesday, December 26, 2007

Garlic1235 wrote to tell me that a chick in her hometown stabbed her boyfriend in the neck with a kitchen knife because he opened one of his Christmas presents early. Garlic found this funny but I don't. I am worried that the dude who got stabbed might be Dan because the chick with the knife sure sounds a whole lot like Martine before her bleeding time. Ha!

LordJCgrl wrote to tell me to stop using OMG in my blog because it offends her as a Christian. I felt really bad. Then I searched and discovered that I had never used OMG once in my whole entire blog! So this chick was calling me out for no reason. OMG, what a righteous, crazy bitch.

Yes, lovelessinAL, I am aware that I type like shit when I am drunk. Are you aware that the reason you are loveless is that you state the obvious like it is insightful?

I am soooooo hungover.

Let me tell you more about the Spooners' party. Workwise I had almost nothing to do because Cole fell asleep pretty soon after I got there. As long as I had the intercom in my hand I was free to do whatever I wanted. Cole only woke up once. I reswaddled him, sang him a few carols and he fell back asleep.

I must have looked extra cute because I got a ton of attention. It didn't hurt that I was the only female there older than 10 and younger than 35 and by far the cutest. I wore my new black velvet dress, my patent leather flats and my new fancy underwear so I felt extra confident. Even Paul told me I looked adorable and he never compliments me on my looks.

I replied "Boy, I sure don't feel it. I hardly slept last night."

"Excitement over Santa's arrival? Or boy trouble?"

It would have been easy to joke and say Santa but I didn't. I said boy trouble.

"Well forget him. You're young and beautiful. You've got your whole life ahead of you. Trust me whoever this punk is, you can do better."

I cannot tell you how happy this made me.

When the party really got started for me was when I got the flamingly gay bartender to fill my half-empty nog glass with pure rum. I got louder and happier and pretty soon all the men started flirting with me. I don't think they expected me to be smart at all, so when I cracked jokes right back at them they loved it. The younger guys were dressed in conservative suits and ties. They all had perky annoying wives except for one who had a tacky implanted girlfriend with big hair and fat lips like she got punched. (I'm sure she deserved it. Ha!) The senior partners kicked it old school in red turtlenecks and double-breasted blazers with sailor buttons. Their ancient wives wore too much makeup on their face-lifts.

The men were gentlemen at first, giving me college advice and laughing loudly at their own jokes but as soon as their wives turned around, a dirty twinkle came into their eyes and they would touch my shoulder for too long and make inappropriate comments. I could practically hear the boners sprouting in their gray flannels. Ha, I say. Ha! It didn't gross me out though. I love being a celebrity.

There was one weird moment I must tell you about even though I'm not sure if it was really weird or I just imagined that it was. Paul entered the kitchen as I was filling the ice bucket. He reached into the freezer to get his special vodka out. Our hands touched. We looked at each other. It was like that famous moment in that French movie Dan showed me where the two fated lovers finally meet. I forget which one. Who's that director? Louch something? Oh, who cares? Fuck Dan. No more Dan. Anyway Paul said something I totally didn't expect.

He said "We have to stop meeting like this. Maggie's getting suspicious."

I didn't know how to take it. I mean I knew it was just a flirty joke but was he trying to tell me something? I didn't know what to say so I decided to pretend that I thought he was totally serious.

I whispered all scared "You're not going to tell her, are you?"

This freaked him out. He turned sort of red, filled up his glass and quickly left. I know what you're thinking. He was just drunk. He made a stupid lame joke and he was embarrassed that I took it seriously. But I know when somebody's joking. He was half joking. Something's going on with him, I can tell. Do I want to know what? No. I just hope he loses Margaret with all his heart. Oh shit. Freudian slip. I meant "loves." But I really mean it. It would be awful if he didn't love her.

Thursday, December 27, 2007

Saturday I'm going to my dad's to celebrate Christmas. I shopped for his present today. I decided to buy him long underwear and heavy socks because his arms and legs get so cold when he goes outside. This is due to the fact that they are concentration-camp skinny with no circulation. While I was at the department store looking, I heard a little girl say "Daddy, isn't this pretty?" I turned around and saw this sweet little black girl holding up a red plaid scarf. Her dad was handsome with a bright smile. He replied "It sure is. In fact it just might be the prettiest scarf I've ever seen."

I know it sounds corny but I got all choked up. It reminded me of when I was little and my dad and I used to do things together. I hid my face in some ski jackets and sort of coughed until I could stop crying. I must have looked like such a freak! Later I walked over and saw the dad standing at the cash register. The little girl was in a big leather chair reading a book. I don't know why but I just had to talk to him. I tapped him on the shoulder and said "Someday when she's all grown-up, she's going to remember when you did things together like this, and she won't be able to stop crying. Nothing's more important to a little girl than time alone with her daddy."

He smiled that big smile and said "The feeling's mutual."

I started crying again. The dude must have thought I was having a nervous breakdown. Hey, maybe I am! Did that ever occur to you, Katherine?

Driving home I called my father to welcome him back from his trip and confirm our plans. Even though I knew it was the last thing he wanted to hear, I told him the story about the man and the little girl in the department store. I just wanted him to know that even though we really aren't friends anymore, deep down I still love him and wish he wasn't dying.

When the story was over, he said "Wait, wait, let me get this straight. You talked to a negro?"

I was so shocked I just sort of stuttered.

He said "Honey, relax, for Christ's sake. It was a joke."

He hurt my feelings and he knew it. I think he felt guilty. He got quiet and said "Yeah when you were little, boy, was I ever your hero. When I got home from work you'd run to the front door. Daaadddy! You'd take me by the hand and lead me to your room. I was the only one you wanted to play with. I was your hero, all right. Then your mom kicked me out. Right before Christmas. You grabbed my leg and wouldn't let go." He laughed and coughed.

"Are you serious?"

"About what?"

"I grabbed your leg?"

"Oh, yeah. You latched on like a pit bull. I dragged you halfway across the lawn. There was a foot of snow too. I was afraid the neighbors were going to call the cops."

"How come you never told me this?"

"It's in the past."

He coughed some more.

I told him I'd see him Saturday.

After I wrapped his present in the last of my Christmas paper (snowflakes on a silver background) I went to my room and cried for a while. Then I slept like a dead person. When I woke up I drank a disturbing amount of caffeine. Then I called Jade and she wasn't home. I texted her and she did not text back. I am starting to truly hate her guts. I was so desperate to go out, I called Fat Merci again but she had plans with high school friends and didn't invite me to come with. I asked her flat out why not, and she said because I get stupid drunk and it's embarrassing. Fine. Fuck it. She's a loser anyway. I didn't tell her that. It's the Christmas season. I just hung up like I could care less. I will never, ever speak to her sloppy fat ass again.

Now I was really desperate so I texted Anton Tuttle and he called me back in six seconds. Remember him? The gamer with the long hair and cute smile who insulted my blog? Well, he couldn't believe I wanted to hang out with him. (Neither could I.) He asked what I wanted to do. I said "Get drunk at your house." He said he had no liquor but he did have some killer weed. I said "Even better." I am going to shave my legs and bikini line now just in case this is the luckiest night of Anton's life.

LATER: 11:47 p.m.

When Anton opened his front door and saw me standing there, he smiled and said "Whoa, no bra."

"Truth in advertising."

"You're pretty smart, you know that?"

"Smart enough to be nice to cute guys with killer weed."

We went downstairs into his basement and proceeded to get thoroughly stoned. I kept wondering if maybe I should have sex with him. It would make him happy and it might be good for my ego to be worshiped again. But then I'd think about Dan and I couldn't go through with it. Our sex was sacred lovemaking. I knew it wouldn't be like that with Anton and maybe not even very fun. Just to make sure, I let him kiss me and take off my shirt. I waited and waited for some feeling to hit me. Nothing. Finally he was moaning and breathing so hard (a form of begging) that I gave him a hand job. It was over superfast and he spurted a ton. Homeboy was due! He said it was my turn now. I said don't bother.

When I got home I went straight to bed but I couldn't sleep. Sad lonely thoughts twisted and turned in my brain. I started wishing I had gone to college because nothing could be worse than this. A very dark place. I got up to blog, hoping it would make me feel better. It hasn't. I feel worse. I should never have let Anton kiss me. I don't even know him or like him.

The TV is telling me all about some Pakistani lady running for president who got shot and killed today. I know I'm supposed to care. I don't care about anything.

Friday, December 28, 2007

I've received many emails asking me why I haven't blogged about Paul Spooner since the Christmas party when he semi-hit on me. Some of you think it's because we are lovers now and I am too afraid to tell you. Boy, do you not know me. If Paul and I were lovers I would need to tell somebody about it and there's no one I trust more than you guys, for the obvious reason that you don't know my real name. Plus I would never be with Paul in a sexual way. Never. I love and respect Margaret way too much. And third, the Spooners have been in Seattle all week visiting Paul's parents. So go wash your filthy minds out with soap. Ha!

Saturday, December 29, 2007

When my dad opened his longjohns and socks today, he smiled like they were joke gifts when in fact they were very high quality expensive items. How can anyone be so ungrateful? Why couldn't I just have a normal father? All he said was "Thanks, kid" then he tossed the box aside without even reading the card. I should be used to behavior like this but I am not. It still hurts.

I gave Affie a sterling silver picture frame so she can frame a pic of my dad and have something to remember him by after he is dead. My mom says I make jokes like this because I think it will make it less painful for me when he actually dies. Maybe, but he does seriously look terminal. The long drive to Affie's mother's house must have been hard on his weakened system. The skin on his face is red and flaky. His yellow-white hair and beard look matted and homeless. His belly has gotten so big it looks like it's ready to explode. And the scariest thing is how frail his voice is. Like a little old lady's. Plus he kept clearing his throat like he's coughing up acid all the time. When I asked him how Christmas was he said "Gunga Din meets Brothers Grimm." I have no idea what this means but it's obviously bad. Please tell me if you understand the joke.

When it was my turn to receive gifts, my dad said "I know what my little girl likes" and handed me an envelope. It was a card of a reindeer peeing "Merry Christmas" in the snow. Inside was a wrinkly hundred-dollar bill. He signed the card "Your #1 fan, Dad." When I pulled the money out I saw that he had recycled an old card. The previous signature was blotted out with sloppy Liquid Paper. What a pathetic example of fathering! Then his dead eyes moved back to the TV where a college bowl game was playing. He absolutely had to watch it because he had a two-hundred-dollar bet. Twice my Christmas present!

Affie gave me a big box of the same stinky Indian incense she gave me last year, which I still haven't used a single stick of, and a wool sweater with animals knitted across the front, which I wouldn't wear even if I was a ten-year-old blind retard going on a field trip to the zoo. As lame as her gifts were, at least she took the time to wrap them.

I wish I understood my father. Every time I tell my mom another one of my theories about why he treats me like shit, she always says the same thing: "He's an alcoholic, honey. It has nothing to do with you. It's a disease. The only thing they love is their next drink." She's probably right. But I still look for theories, I can't help it. I wonder if maybe I don't build up his ego enough with compliments. Or maybe he thinks if I was never born my mother wouldn't have kicked him out. Or maybe my face and body look so much like my mom's when she was young that it freaks him out to be around me. It's like a ghost or something. A ghost he used to bone! Or maybe he is afraid that if he felt true fatherly love for me it would remind him of the good old days when we were a family, and his heart would break in two. Or maybe my mom is right and he loves only his next drink and hates everything else, including me and the drink he's holding in his hand.

Driving home to face another Saturday night alone, I did something stupid. I visited Elysium Books. Don't worry, I didn't go in. I'm not that self-destructive. I just stood outside and watched Glenn A. Warburg through the window ringing up a purchase. The window was decorated with holly, pine branches and old leather books stacked on a little antique stepladder. Maybe Glenn is gay. How many straight men decorate like that? I really wanted to enter and say hello. I knew we would have a wonderful conversation and that he would give me brilliant transcendent advice about Dan. Then he would butt-rape me. Just kidding! God, relaaax! Next I stopped at a liquor store that just opened and tried to buy some wine coolers. Even though I flirted with the cute Asian emo behind the counter he said no way, not without a better fake I.D. Because I still haven't activated my Netflix, I then stopped at Blockbuster and rented an oldie but a goodie called *Random Harvest*. It is a film that Dan and I watched a lot of one night. After we fooled around, he told me all about one of the actresses in the movie, a gorgeous girl named Susan Peters and how she was nominated for an Oscar for the movie but then a few years later was paralyzed from the waist down in a hunting accident. She got a few more acting jobs in a wheelchair but then became so depressed, she starved herself to death when she was like 30. The story of Susan Peters was so sad that ever since, I've wanted to see the movie all the way through. Tonight was the perfect night to do it because I was in the mood to let all my emotions out. Boy, did it work. I had to pause the movie about 50 times while I cried and cried. My mom overheard me and came in. She said obviously I should work in the film business one day. Movies were clearly my bliss.

"No," I thought, "Dan is."

I wish I had amnesia and then suddenly remembered that I have a soul mate I had totally forgotten about. How great would that be?

Tuesday, January 1, 2008

Anton invited me to a New Year's Eve party at his parents' house but I told him I was too devastated to party. He asked by what. I said "Man trouble. It's like boy trouble only way more interesting." It was a bitchy thing to say so soon after I fooled around with him but I wanted him to know that what happened between us was a one-time thing. Maybe if I weren't so messed up psychologically he would be a perfect boyfriend for me but what am I supposed to do, pretend I'm mentally healthy when I am so obviously not?

My mom was annoyed that I rejected his invitation because she and Mark wanted the house to themselves so they could bone by the fireplace. Of course she didn't say that but I know the woman. Since they were stuck with me, they gracefully invited me to join their candlelight steak dinner. I ate as fast as I could then escaped upstairs with half a bottle of champagne.

To drown out the sounds of their passion, I turned on the TV New Year's Eve festivities. But I didn't watch. I chatted online, with other lost souls who were home alone on the biggest party night of the year. I was probably the only one in the chat room who was not fat, stinky and in a wheelchair. Ha! At midnight I planned to give myself a big wet kiss in the mirror and go straight to sleep. That's all I wanted. Peace and quiet. I had no idea what was about to take place. If I had I probably would have jumped out the window.

. . .

My mom knocked on my door two minutes before twelve. I assumed it was to give me a holiday hug and kiss good night. But she was crying her ass off. Mark was standing right behind her and he was sniffling too. Before I could say anything, she held up her hand and showed me a big tacky diamond ring.

I know I should be grateful that my middle-aged mom, cursed for life with tharm and cankle and emotional saddle baggage, has found a man who loves her so much he wants to marry her, but I am not. Mark Aubichon is not good enough for her by a mile. The only reason she said yes to his proposal is that she has low self-esteem and is afraid to be alone. I swear, if it would stop her from marrying him I would skip college and stay home.

I faked joy and gave my mom a big loving hug. Mark tried to hug me too but I ran right past him to get more champagne which I desperately needed. I came back pretty fast and while all the celebrators on TV honked horns and screamed, we stood around toasting their marriage like it was the greatest event since mankind landed on the moon. I deserve an award for how happy I pretended to be.

As soon as I got rid of them, I chugged the last drops of my champagne and got my emergency joint out of my underwear drawer. It is truly for emergencies only. I sat down on the window seat and said to myself "Time to sleep forever, Katie." It was freezing out and starting to snow. I opened the window and just as I lifted the lighter to put the worst New Year's Eve out of its misery, my phone rang.

Was it Dan? I grabbed it and looked. Just Rory. If it hadn't been for my mom's big announcement I would definitely have let it go to voice mail, but since Rory hates Mark's guts way more than I do, I knew he would be sympathetic. When I picked up, the music and voices were so loud in the background I couldn't understand a word he was saying. Then I realized he was crying. I thought maybe his mom with M.S. had finally died, but then I heard him say Jade's name. I yelled into the phone that I couldn't understand him. He moved outside and that's when he told me the story that made my horrible night even worse.

He said that after we broke up, he took two Ambien and fell asleep crying. Jade was over at the time, downloading a new bum-fights video she wanted Willy to watch. Right in the middle of watching it, she excused herself, walked down the hall and got into bed with Rory. When he woke up she was blowing him. He tried to stop her but he was too drugged. She finished and totally swallowed.

In the morning he hoped it was just a bad dream but when he opened his eyes there she was, sleeping naked. He woke her up and said that he still loved me and wanted to get back together and that she should get dressed and go home. She acted like she could care less and left. But the very next night she came back with hash. They smoked it and have been together ever since. There is no DJ named J.D. She made him up to deceive me.

When I didn't react or say anything, Rory assumed I was crushed and he started blubbering again. He said that he and Jade just had the hugest fight ever. She accused him of still being in love with me and he didn't deny it. She went crazy and threatened to call me up and say it was all his fault that they hooked up because he practically raped her and that ever since, she has been too afraid to dump him. Rory begged me not to believe her lies. He said he wished he'd never gotten near her and that she is pure evil. I still didn't say anything. My head and heart were completely blank. It was like I was trapped inside a dream that had nothing to do with me.

"Are you there, baby?" he said.

"Uh-huh."

He started crying harder and begged me to forgive him. This is my all-time least favorite quality in a guy. If you're going to cheat, fine, but don't whine about it. Man up. Admit you wanted that pussy. The more he cried the more I hated him. When I couldn't take it anymore I hung up in his face, switched my phone to vibrate and threw it on the bed. I did not cry. I was like "Okay, guys are shit. I knew this. This is not news." What I did with Dan was wrong but what Rory did with Jade was worse. He boned my best and only friend. And no way was he a victim. A guy only gets hard if wants to.

Even though it was about ten degrees out, I opened the window as high as it can go. The snow was falling harder. Big and flaky. It landed on my lap. I smoked my entire emergency joint that way, slamming back each toke as far as I could and holding it for as long as possible. When I was done I hissed the roach on the window sill. My knuckles were dark red and semi-paralyzed. I closed the window and climbed into bed with all my clothes on. I was shivering and the ceiling was spinning. I was so high! I let my troubles spin spin spin away. I fell asleep but not deeply. All night I could hear my phone vibrating. I didn't care what Rory or Jade had to say. I knew I would never speak to either one of them again. Let it snow, let it snow, let it snow!

Today my mom cooked a special roast beef dinner which I ate way too much of. We toasted their engagement again but this time with sparkling cider which made it harder to pretend I was enthusiastic. During dessert Mark asked why Jade hadn't joined us and I said she was in the hospital with full-blown AIDS.

"That's not funny," my mom said.

"That's terrible," Mark added.

I replied "Even worse for the monkey she blew to get it."

I was excused.

Phone ringing. Somebody loves me. Stand by.

. . .

It was Joel Seidler, my old geometry tutor, who I never call back. This time I picked up and we conversated (as the sistas say) for half an hour. Turns out the poor kid has some serious mental issues. He has family problems like everybody else (a Jewish dad who wants him to be a lawyer no matter what and a crazy Jewish mom who'd still be wiping his butt if he let her), but he says the reason for his depression is purely biochemical. It began in high school, got worse and worse every year, and by the time school started this year he could barely get out of bed. He finally went to the Princeton shrink, and even though it was a relief to talk to somebody about his parents, it didn't make him any less depressed. When he started to call suicide hotlines just for the fun of it, his shrink put him on major meds. A few days later one of his roommates caught him trying to jump off the roof of the dorm. Princeton sent him home. Now he's seeing a doctor here who has put him on different meds. He's not doing great but he's definitely better.

The reason he called is because he heard I deferred college, and since we both have mental health issues he knew we would have a lot to talk about. (Everybody knows about my three days in the psych ward.) I told him I was really busy with my new job and my mom's engagement, but as soon as things cleared up I would definitely give him a call. This was a lie. I don't think I should be spending time with someone who has more problems than I do.

. . .

Longest post ever. The Spooners' vacation is over. I can't wait to see them tomorrow. I've missed them so much!

LATER: 3:42 a.m.

Can't sleep. Can't stop thinking about everything. Total nightmare.

FYI to Ukpjohnson: Bum fights are real-life videos of home-less men beating the crap out of each other in exchange for cash or alcohol. They are the favorite of Filipino whores.

Wednesday, January 2, 2008

When Margaret asked me how my vacation was I told her what happened with Rory and Jade. She said really sweet things about how I was a wonderful girl who deserved much better treatment. I told her that my New Year's resolution was never to speak to either one of them again.

"You go, girl," she said, acting all street and snapping her fingers.

I asked her if she had made any resolutions and she said "Yes, I'm going back to work part-time."

"Wow. That's a big deal, right?"

"It depends on your point of view. I don't think so but Paul does. If he had his way I'd stay home forever. I'd be a broodmare."

I just assumed a broodmare was some sort of sad horse, but it turns out it's a horse that does nothing but give birth. I guess Paul wants more kids and Margaret doesn't. I find this surprising because Margaret is such an excellent mother. But she is exhausted most of time and has big rings under her eyes because Cole nurses so much at night.

Paul came home for lunch while Margaret was upstairs with Cole. He gave me a pat on the back and said he felt terrible about what Rory had done to me, but that he was also relieved that it was a boy that had made me so depressed and not my job. He had been afraid that I was unhappy working for them and that I was about to quit. Which would have been awful, he said, because they adore me and trust me completely with Cole. What a kind thing to say! Why can't my dad be like this? I was dying to tell him the real reason for my unhappiness (Dan not Rory) but I thought it might freak him out to know that his nanny was romantically involved with someone almost as old as he is.

I said "Are you kidding? I love my job. And I adore you too." I meant to say "adore you guys too." No big deal, right? Well it was. Paul smiled at me in a weird way. Then I remembered the awkward moment from the party after our hands touched and I thought "Whoa, does he have a crush on me?" I started blushing. Then Margaret walked in burping Cole. Paul sort of twitched like he had been caught doing something he shouldn't.

Margaret said "What's wrong?"

"What do you mean?" Paul replied.

"You're so jumpy."

"Too much coffee."

Thursday, January 3, 2008

A friend from high school emailed just now to say that my old locker partner, Lori McMurrin, and her two 13-year-old twin sisters shroomed together in Grove Street Park on New Year's Day. Afterwards the twins were goofing around on the hood of Lori's car when she pulled out of the parking lot. Brilliant, right? Lori saw a police car and without thinking she slammed the brakes way too hard. One sister held on but the other one flew off and cracked her head on the curb and died.

When you spend all day taking care of a baby you really understand what a nightmare this is. You understand how much love and attention went into that girl every single day and night for 13 years and for what? All gone now. If I were Lori's mother I'd beat the shit out of Lori for being such a fucking dummy. And she goes to Tufts! You'd think all that college structure would have made her smarter than the kid who cleans the apple-pie machine at McDonald's.

The Iowa elections are on TV. This handsome skinny black dude running named Barrack Obama reminds me very much of Jimmy Stewart. It looks like he could win. How awesome would that be? A brutha as president. And guess what? I can finally vote!

Whenever I used to speak in questions like "How cool is that?" or "How much do we love her?" Dan would always say back "How rhetorical are you?" I didn't get the joke until he explained it. You have to admit it's pretty genius.

Paul didn't come home for lunch today and I was too embarrassed to ask Margaret why not. I hope it was because he got busy and not because he feels uncomfortable around me now that I told him I adore him. Which I do!

Friday, January 4, 2008
Joel Seidler called again and asked if I was tired of blowing him off yet. I told him as a matter of fact I was. Ha! We met at Pete's Italian Kitchen, the best place in town to double the size of one's ass. Joel looked pretty much the way I remembered him—short and dumpy with pasty pale skin,

tiny eyes hiding behind a gigantic nose, and birthing hips. The only change I noticed was that his eye-rings are blacker and he has started smoking. Which I friggin' love! We sat outside under heat lamps and chained our lungs into submission. Last one to cancer is a rotten egg!

I told Joel all about my life. The tragic part with Dan and the pathetic part with Rory. Joel is just as good a listener today as he was in high school. When I was done talking, he leaked some smoke out of his big ole nose and said "Huh."

I laughed and said "What does that mean?"

"It means I think you need to forget about romance for a while and concentrate on getting your shit together. It might take a while."

"Oh, come on. Everybody's life is a hot mess at my age."

"Sure, but to get better you need some awareness. I'm profoundly screwed up but at least I know it. You have no clue."

"Am I really that bad?"

"Oh, yeah."

It was weird hearing this from someone I respect. I got paranoid for a second and wondered if he was just saying this to tear down my self-confidence so I'd let him bone me. In high school he called me his "shiksa goddess" and sometimes when I was too nice to him, his face would turn red and I could practically hear the sperms squirting into his undies. But things never got awkward between us because he knew he didn't have a chance. I flicked my ash and asked him in what way I was messed up exactly.

"I don't know. I'm not a psychiatrist. Have you ever been in therapy?"

"Only in eighth grade."

"Maybe you should start up again."

I scribbled in the air with my cigarette. "Waiter? Check?"

This cracked him up.

When we said goodbye in the parking lot, Joel said "Take care" in a serious way, like he really meant it. I felt guilty I hadn't asked him anything about himself all night. He's the one who almost jumped off a dorm not me. But I did pay for the dinner so I'm not completely selfish.

Something ironic: I have no real friends left but in the past day, 3852 discrete viewers have read my blog and 32 sent me email. Only on the internet can a person be lonely and popular at the same time.

Saturday, January 5, 2008

Here is another chance to get to know me better. You will never regret it!

Q. Have you ever been searched by the cops?

A. Yes, they found a pussy in my pocket.

Q. Have you ever tried heroin?

A. Once. I fell asleep.

Q. Which do you prefer, the top or the bottom?

A. Bottom if I trust the guy, top if I don't.

Q. Do you believe in the horoscope?

A. Sagittarians never do.

Q. Which is more advanced, your creativity or your memory?

A. Both are fairly genius but I would have to say— Wait, what's the question again?

Q. Do you stay friends with your exes?

A. Only if they can handle being around me platonically. So far it's not happened.

Q. If you're stopped at a red light at two a.m. and no one is around to see you, do you run the light?

A. No way. I am scared of authority.

Q. What's the main thing on your mind these days?

A. Sex with Dan. Just once more. Paleeeze!

Q. Do you pee in swimming pools?

A. That's the only place.

There are many more questions, but I will stop here. You're welcome.

Sunday, January 6, 2008

This is going to sound insanely superficial but I love Cole and no matter how much he cries or how many times he poos, I am always happy to take care of him but what if he wasn't drop dead gorgeous? What if he was butt-fugly? Would I still love him as much? What do parents do when their babies are hideous? What happens?

Cole already looks like a gorgeous little jock. His shoulders are broad and he has the cutest bubble butt. Paul was a wrestler in high school. I've never dated a jock. Which is unusual. Usually the prettiest girl in school dates the sports hero but I've always preferred brains over brawn. Paul has both. Lucky Margaret!

Monday, January 7, 2008

This morning at approximately 8:30 a.m. I was brushing my teeth, thinking about nothing, when my phone rang. It came up restricted. The only person I know with a blocked number is my dad. I answered anyway. It was Affie crying so hard that she could barely talk. Affie never cries. The more pain she is in, the bigger she smiles. I sat down on the toilet seat and waited for the terrible words.

"Your father, he . . . he . . . he slipped on the ice! He fell down the back steps! A terrible fall!"

My dad's apartment is on the second floor and has wooden steps in back. I stayed calm and asked what happened. She said he slipped on the icy steps on his way down to the garbage cans and cracked his skull open. They rushed him to St. Francis around midnight for surgery. He is in a coma now. Could I come down right away? Nope, sorry, Affie, too busy.

Of course I could come! Dumb-ass!

I ran downstairs to tell my mom but she was gone for an early dentist appointment. I sort of panicked and ran around for a while, up and down the stairs for no reason. When I was finally on my way to the hospital I realized I had forgotten to put on my coat. I turned the heat on full blast and cranked up the ass warmer. Then I was like "Oh, yeah, I have a job." I called Paul, told him what happened and said I'd be late for work.

"No, Katie, you're not going to be late. You won't be coming in at all. What's happened to your dad is serious. Take as many days as you need."

That's when it hit me and I started crying.

"Oh, sweetheart," he said. "I'm so sorry you have to go through this. Call me if you need anything."

He was so kind I started balling harder. I hung up and called my mom, but she didn't pick up. She was still in the dentist's chair. I texted her what happened. Pulling into the sunny hospital parking lot I thought "Wait, how could my dad slip on ice? There isn't any." It hit me that Affie was lying. He slipped because he was drunk! Affie constantly protects him which is the main reason he keeps her around. Once while she was pouring him like his twentieth beer of the day, I said "You know he's an alcoholic, right?" She replied "All I know is that lately he's the happiest I've ever seen him." Happy with a liver the size of a basketball? Whatever, crazy lady.

My mom called as I was getting into the elevator and she was a total wreck. This surprised me because I always thought she stopped loving my dad about two seconds after I was born. She said she wanted so badly to come to the hospital but it would be unfair to Affie. Which is true. My dad's still in love with my mom. Affie knows it.

When I walked into the waiting room, the first thing I saw was a demented street person. It took me a few seconds to realize it was Affie, wearing gray sweats, pink fuzzy slippers and a Greenbay Packers T-shirt. She wore no makeup and her hair looked stiff and dead. She ran over to me. Her eyes were bulging. She whispered "If they ask, say that we're married or they won't let me see him!" Before I could say don't worry, a doctor walked up and introduced himself. His name was Dr. David Clarkson. Sweet smile, soft voice, bald but not old.

On the way in to see my dad, Dr. Clarkson warned me that he was in "grave condition" and to prepare myself for the worst. I tried to but I failed. I could not believe how bad my dad looked! His whole head was wrapped in bandages and he was surrounded by tubes and machines. (Thank god Aunt Dorothea pays his medical insurance!) Dr. Clarkson said that when he fell an artery in the sack around his brain ripped open and started to bleed. The surgeon managed to "evacuate the clog" and stop the bleeding, but right now there was nothing else they could do for him. I'm not sure what I replied. When he turned away, I walked over and touched my dad's wrinkly little hand. It was burning hot. His eyelids were twitching like he was dreaming. Of what? The magical day I was born? The day he taught me to ride a bike? A cold beer?

I whispered "You in there, Daddy? Can you hear me?"

As usual, no reaction.

In the afternoon Dr. Yi, who Clarkson said is one of the best neurologists in the country, took me and Affie into a little room where they had my dad's scans all lit up on a box. He showed us where the blood was. It looked like a big white hurricane near the middle of his head that was squishing his brain into the sides of his skull. I asked if they could drain the blood somehow, and he said that was impossible because it would destroy too much of his brain. He said right now they were just hoping his vital signs would get better. He said to page him anytime if we had questions or needed to talk. I started to cry. He gave me a few pats on the back.

They kicked us out at 8:00 p.m. When I got home my mom forced me to eat macaroni and cheese and I went straight to bed. I was so wiped out I was sure I'd fall over like a sawed tree. Instead I just laid there staring up at the ceiling. My heart beat so fast it hurt. Even though I've known his death was coming for a long time, I'm not ready to lose my dad forever.

I got up to write all this down. Not just for you guys but so someday my kids can learn how their grampy died.

It's 2:23 now. I am so tired I feel like throwing up. I have to be at the hospital first thing. There's nothing worse than having insomnia when you know you have to get up early the next day. Wish me luck.

LATER: 4:38 a.m.

Your wishes didn't work. I figure it is better to be typing than staring at the ceiling. I just emailed Paul to tell him I wouldn't be coming in tomorrow. I also googled "fractured skull" and "brain hemorrhages." That was fun. Now I am sleepy again, but I know that as soon as I turn off the lights I will feel wide awake. Torture!

It's snowing outside. The sky is black. Usually snow on the ground makes me happy. Right now it seems creepy and dangerous. Like a murderer is out there waiting.

I'm not religious but if you are, please pray for a miracle, because that's the only thing that will save my dad. Oh and one more thing. If your father is still alive, even if he is a major fuck-up, call him and tell him you love him. Even if you think you don't mean it.

Tuesday, January 8, 2008

I was about to leave for the hospital when I got the feeling that my father was already dead. I called and the nurse told me he was the same so there was no need to hurry. I drank an obscene amount of coffee and devoured two bowls of oatmeal with bananas. Then I answered some of your emails. Just the sweet thoughtful ones. Now it is time for me to go again.

The worst email I got teased me for writing "balling" instead of "bawling." Did you really think it was necessary to correct my spelling when my father is dying? I will say it again. I am the world's worst speller. If spell-check misses it, then so do I!

LATER: 10:18 p.m.

The longest day ever at the hospital. My dad got another scan. Dr. Clarkson said his condition is "very grave." He is negative and repetitious. I am starting to dislike him. Affie was beyond insane. Shouldn't I be the one going insane? I might lose my father, the only one I'll ever have. Affie is losing a decrepit drunk boyfriend who stunk up her apartment and treated her like an annoying slave. Affie whines nonstop and talks about him like he's some sort of genius who would have written amazing sports biographies if only he hadn't been cursed with a bad wife and a weak liver. I reminded her that his liver wouldn't have been weak if he hadn't drunk three six-packs a day his whole life. She says I know nothing about depression and how terrible it is to be married to a woman who castrates you. I wanted to reply that my mom only castrated him because he hardly ever worked and cheated on her like a thousand times. But I didn't. Somebody has to be mature.

In the afternoon Affie found an Indian doctor she trusted named Dr. V. D. Ghosh. He is tall, skinny, married and handsome. He put my dad on a different antibiotic. He says his condition is "velly glave."

All day I kept thinking how amazing it is that a body as devastated as my dad's can survive this long. Imagine if he had taken care of himself. He might have lived to be 108 instead of 54.

Dr. Ghosh asked if my father had ever signed papers indicating his wishes in circumstances like these. In other words did he want the plug pulled? Affie said softly and calmly that there were no papers that she was aware of. But the second he left the room, she freaked out and dug her nails into my arm. Her crazy eyes were as big as walnuts. "You must promise me, little girl, that you will never let them kill your father, no matter what! No matter what!"

I felt like punching her in the dot. I told her that as far as I was concerned they were legally married so it was totally her decision. Like that's a choice I would ever want to make about my own dad!

Thank you for all your prayers. I hope somebody up there hears them. I doubt it but you never know.

LATER: 1:08 a.m.

Before I went to bed I called the Spooners to update them on my dad's condition. I assumed I would get their voice mail, but Paul picked up and we talked for over an hour. He really made me laugh telling me stories about the temp nanny they hired to replace me. Her name is Alma and she is sweet but really dense. Cole is teaching her the alphabet! He said they miss me terribly and that when I am not there it's like a day without sunshine. It is wonderful to be appreciated.

Paul also informed me that Barrack Obama lost the New Hampshire primary election today. It turns out we both really like him and want him to be president. I asked if this means Hillary will win now.

He said "Not by a long shot."

I said "I'm sorry if it makes me a bad feminist or something, but her ass scares the crap out of me."

He laughed and said "That's how I feel about her husband."

Friday, January 11, 2008

I'm sorry I haven't had a chance to answer any of your recent letters. My father died Wednesday morning at 2:26 a.m.

Affie called and said "He's gone, Katie. He's gone." She wasn't crying at all, which was weird, because that's all she'd been doing since the accident. Maybe her religion has taken over and she is happy knowing that any second now he will return as a moth or a raccoon.

In a way I am relieved he's dead. I am sorry if that sounds harsh, but I knew he wasn't going to get better, and there was no way Affie would have had the courage to pull the plug. I could not have done it either. Not to my one and only dad. So it's probably better that he died peacefully this way rather than live on as a vegetable.

The viewing wake is in one hour. I have heard that it is a good thing to have an open coffin because it makes the death more real. Otherwise, if you never actually see the corpse, you dream about the person for years to come. In your dreams they are always alive and you realize that you were misinformed and that they never really died. When you wake up and discover that you were only dreaming, it messes you up for days.

LATER: 11:57 p.m.

An open coffin is the most heinous thing ever. My father looked like the shriveled puppet version of himself. I don't know if they drained his belly or what, but it was totally flat, and the brown corduroy suit they put him in was about three sizes too big. They removed his head bandages, but to cover up the surgery scar and shaved head they put him in a weird gray wig and the stupid hat he wore whenever he went to the horse track. When I walked up to the coffin I knew everyone was staring at me so I didn't let on how grotesque I thought he looked. I knew this was the last time I would ever see him. His brown-yellow fingernails were dried and cracked. There was a tiny bit of white hair on his Adam's apple that they missed when they trimmed his beard. One of his cuff links was on backwards or maybe his sleeve had just gotten twisted around. I leaned down, pulled back the brim of his hat and kissed his forehead. It was cold, like kissing a marble statue in the winter. Your dad is your big hero and then one day he is a freezing puppet lying in a box. Wow, life sure is charming.

For the funeral I can't decide between my black dress or my other black dress. I think I'll go with my black dress. Boo hoo.

Sunday, January 13, 2008

The funeral was better than the wake because the coffin was closed and people got up and spoke. Mitch Massey, my dad's editor at the last magazine where he worked until he was fired for being a drunk, said my dad was the funniest man he ever met. He said he would have liked to share with us some of the wittiest things he said but he couldn't because there were ladies present. Everyone cracked up because they knew what a foul pig my dad was. To give you an example, Affie has this wooden box where she keeps all the seeds for her porch garden. One day she came in all worried because by accident she had left it out many nights in a row. She said "Oh no, there's cobwebs in my seed box!" And he said back really fast "Oh, come on, Affie, it hasn't been that long since we fucked."

Mitch also said my dad was a magical writer. He said when my dad wrote about a sporting event you felt like you were there. And if you actually were there, his story was even better than the actual experience. A huge compliment for a writer.

It's hard to cry at a funeral when you are the only child and everyone is staring at you.

Next was my great-uncle Roger from Rhode Island who I had never met. He is the brother of Aunt Dorothea. He flew in to represent that entire side of the family. He shared memories of how delightful and cute my dad was when he was little. He didn't have to say it, but we all knew that when my dad started drinking that pretty much put an end to it.

When Affie got up I was sure it was going to be the most embarrassing experience of my life, but she was amazingly cool. She told stories about my dad like he was the sexiest man alive. How he swept her off her feet, how romantic he was and sensitive and kind, and how he opened up a whole new world of love for her. It was just a fantasy but since it was the same one I had when I was little, it made me happy to believe in it again for a few minutes.

I spoke last. I hadn't really planned anything. I thanked everyone for coming and said that I had fond memories of my dad and that I would always cherish them. I told about the time when he woke me up in the middle of the night when I was about five because there was a Marx Brothers movie on TV he wanted me to see. I loved Harpo and thought my dad was pretty amazing to go to all the trouble of waking me up. I also shared how I used to pour beers for him and that as politically incorrect as it was, it made me feel very important, and that to this day I am an expert on how to pour so the foam doesn't spill over. People laughed at this. I then told everyone about this game my dad and I used to play when we were watching TV together. I would tell him I wanted a sip of his beer and when he reached to get his mug I would flop down and make a raspberry sound on his beer belly. He would pretend to get really mad, like I had tricked him into it, and I would laugh my ass off. Even though this is sort of a sad story because it involves alcohol, everyone knew I was being honest and that this was the sort of person he was. I didn't cry once the whole time I spoke and neither did almost anyone else. That is what I wanted.

Before the final prayer a beautiful woman stood up and sang a song called "Turn, Turn, Turn." The lyrics are beautiful and say something like there is a time to work, a time to play, a time to plant, a time to sew, a time for every single thing under heaven. These words reminded me of how big life is and that individuals live and die and that it was my dad's turn to die and now it is my turn to live. I finally started to cry a little. My mom was really sweet, hugging me and giving me tissues, and whispering that she loved me. If Mark hadn't been sitting right next to her, holding her hand with the giant diamond on it, I would have said I loved her back.

When we got home my mom and Mark wanted to take me out for a nice dinner. I said I was too tired but that they should definitely go without me. Two minutes after they left I fell asleep with all my black clothes on.

Today all I did was smoke and sleep.

There was one thing the priest said that I really liked. "Naked I came from my mother's womb and naked I shall return." It made me feel like my father was happy and safe now. I want that written on my tombstone. Hint hint. ☺

Monday, January 14, 2008

My first day back. Boy, were the Spooners happy to see me. Even Cole clapped. During lunch Paul and I had a first-rate conversation. That's one of Paul's favorite words. First-rate. He uses it all the time. His other favorite words are non-starter, sublime, insipid and paradox. I am a total sponge and am already starting to use them. We talked mostly about our fathers. Paul's dad was a huge jock at Stanford. A really nasty dude, sounds like. He used to tease Paul because Paul didn't like any sports except wrestling. In high school Paul was president of his class and a member of the chess club, math club and bridge club. I just love how the kids who were the brainiacs in high school grow up to be such remarkable men and how the football players end up managing Jiffy Lubes. That's what Paul says anyway.

Paul can't believe how fine I seem with my dad's death. I explained that he had been sick for a very long time so I'd pretty much prepared myself for it. He smiled and said that young people are so arrogant. I started to get defensive and he said no, it's a good thing because if we weren't so arrogant we would be in big trouble. I asked him to explain. He said it is the arrogance of youth that allows us to make the difficult transition to adulthood. It allows us to take risks, fight for idealistic causes, fall in love, start impossible careers, etc.

I asked him what arrogance has to do with that. He said young people think they know everything when they actually know very little. Adults try to talk sense to us but we ignore them because we think grown-ups are full of shit and that their advice is based on their own failed lives and that we are going to do so much better than they did. Paul said that although this is frustrating for adults it is actually a good thing because if young people understood how cruel and complicated life truly is, they might crawl into their basement with a crack pipe and never come out.

"You mean life is worse than I think?"

"Much. For instance, you think you're okay with your dad's death? Not a chance. The hardest decade of life will be your thirties. If you're really lucky you'll fall apart completely, finally deal with your dad's death and every other heartbreak you've ever had, and then you'll put yourself back together again. If you're unlucky you won't fall apart. You'll stay in denial and grow into a sad old person with hemorrhoids, clogged arteries and cancer."

"Awesome."

He laughed.

Then I said "I always thought the hardest part of life was supposed to be right after college. When you have to figure out what you want to do with your life."

"Nope. That child's play compared to your thirties."

"Tell me more about life and how it's going to be. I'll believe you, I promise. I won't be arrogant."

"Sorry. I've got to get back to work."

Fascinating boss, right?

Tuesday, January 15, 2008

When Cole was born his eyes were blue but now they are on their way to brown. Margaret was hoping they'd stay blue so she could see herself in him. I told her I would see her in Cole no matter what color his eyes were. This made her really happy. But to be honest the browner his eyes get, the more he looks like Paul. I hardly see any of Margaret in Cole anymore.

I was watching a soap opera on the floor with Cole lying next to me on his mat. I gave him my pinkie and thumb and he grabbed on with both hands and yanked and wrestled with them for like 15 minutes. Boy is he strong. And the whole time he kicked, kicked, kicked with joy.

"Look at my happy kid!" Paul said when he saw us sitting there. "Can you blame him? He gets to hold hands with a gorgeous girl all day!"

So I'm gorgeous, huh? Verrry interesting.

Wednesday, January 16, 2008

I called Dan just now to tell him that my dad died. The first two times Martine answered and I hung up. The third time Dan answered on the first ring.

I said "Hi, it's me. I have something important to tell you."

He said "I'm sorry you have the wrong number. Please stop bothering us."

He hung up in my face.

He's lucky I don't send Martine a long letter.

Thursday, January 17, 2008

Today I was eating lunch while Paul read the *Wall Street Journal.* I started complaining about how my mom is getting married to a jerk and how she expects me to be the maid of honor. I went on bitching for about five minutes. Finally Paul said "It could be worse. You could be one of the seven Iraqis blown up yesterday by a suicide bomber." Many people would find a comment like this annoying but I didn't. I like that Paul doesn't take me too seriously. Rory would have spent an hour listening to me bitch until I lost all respect for him. Dan would have psychoanalyzed me and hurt my feelings. But Paul, saying what he said, let me know I was acting like a spoiled brat and that there were way worse things in the world than my stupid problems. I think the only reason

I complain around Paul is to have something passionate to talk about.

Later Paul explained the way our primary elections work, which makes no sense, but he said there are many, many things in our democratic system that make no sense, and yet it's still better than any other system. He also explained the difference between Republicans and Democrats.

Republicans say "Screw the poor, let's keep all the money for ourselves."

Democrats say "No, let's keep almost all the money for ourselves and give the poor just enough so they don't start a revolution and cut our heads off."

Twice during our political talk I made him crack up. The first was when I said that Barrack Obama is black Jimmy Stewart. Paul laughed and said "Perfect, perfect!" The second was when we were talking about Hillary and I said no way would I vote for a president with tharm and cankle.

"I don't know what that is," Paul replied.

"Thigh-arm and calf-ankle."

He howled.

It's wonderful making him laugh.

Margaret is very serious. I don't know if it's because she is always so exhausted from breastfeeding or if that's just how she is.

. . .

I still can't believe Dan hung up on me like I was some annoying twat raising money for sick kids in baseball hats to go to Disneyland. When he finds out that my dad died, he's going to feel soooooo guilty!

I saw a funny little man interviewed on TV who wrote a book that claims that in the future people will have sex with their own personal robots and even fall in love with them. I don't think I would like to have a robot programmed to love me. Why not? you ask. Because one of the most exciting things about getting a guy is knowing that he could be with many other girls but chose me.

Saturday, January 19, 2008

After my last blog I couldn't stand being cooped up any more so I stole three of Mark's Dutch beers, got in my car and drove around in the snow drinking them. Then all of the sudden I was on the highway heading to Dan's house. Maybe deep down that's where I was going the whole time but I couldn't admit it to myself. Everything was dark when I got there except for a light on the second floor. I assumed it was either Dan's office or their bedroom. If it was his office, maybe he was up working late and Martine was sleeping. If it was the bedroom, maybe they were both awake watching TV.

I knocked. No one came. I knocked louder. "What's the

worst that can happen?" I kept thinking, without once actually trying to answer the question. If I had answered the question I would have run to my car and driven away like Danica Patrick. Just when I was sure that no one was home, the door opened fast and there was this beautiful woman standing before me. She looked maybe 30. Short black hair and perfect white skin. Thick pouty lips. She was wearing boxers and a big T-shirt from Dan's college. She held a textbook in her hand and her glasses were pushed up onto her head. A total Jade body, tiny and strong. Her nipples were visible through her T-shirt. She looked annoyed and curious but mostly curious.

"Hi, my name's Patty Marvin. I'm a student of Professor Gallo's. I hate to interrupt you but I need to talk to him. It's really, really important."

"I'm zorry," she said. "He's not 'ome."

"Damn! Are you sure?"

"Of courz I am sewer."

I grumbled to myself like a crazy person then I turned and ran away. The walk was really icy. I slipped and landed right on my ass. I was too embarrassed to look back so I got up and kept running. In the middle of the street, I tripped forward and landed on both hands. When I got to my car I spun around on the ice and yelled "I just found out I have Hep C, so I'm not going to be able to turn in my assignment on time!" Before she could say anything I jumped in and drove away. I wanted her to think I was some bipolar student. To show up at a professor's house in the middle of the night you'd sort of have to be insane, right?

Yesterday when I woke up I could not believe what I had done. It didn't feel real. It was like some thriller I had seen the night before. No way I actually starred in it! But one look at my scraped hands proved I was wrong. In the shower, as I was wondering why I did it and thanking god I didn't get busted, I looked down and saw that my period had started. No wonder! How did I not figure that out? It was the hormones, baby!

There was only one thing that never occurred to me. Once upon a time I gave Dan a photograph of me as a present. It was from when my mom took me to Puerto Rico on vacation. I was wearing a bikini and posing like a beach bunny. When I gave it to Dan he grinned and said "If you weren't jailbait, I'd frame this." He gave it back. It really hurt my feelings so when it was time for me to go, I secretly slipped it into one of his photo albums. What I didn't know was that a few weeks later he and Martine were looking through the album together and she found the photo. She asked who it was. Dan panicked for a sec, then said it was his second cousin Fiona from Oregon.

How do I know this? you ask. Because when I was driving to work yesterday Dan called me screaming. I wasn't even sure it was him at first he sounded so different. He called me a psychotic bitch and told me to stay out of his life forever. I was so shocked I didn't even talk. I just pulled over by the train tracks and started crying. Finally when he got tired of calling me names I said I was really sorry and that I would never have come by his house if he hadn't hung up on me and that the only reason I called in the first place was to tell him that my father died.

Silence.

Boy, did he feel guilty! He said he was truly deeply sorry for my loss. I thanked him and said it was the hardest thing I had ever gone through. (Ha!) I asked him how he knew it was me who came by and that was when he told me about Martine and the photo album. It turns out that when she opened the door she recognized me immediately and didn't believe for one second that I was his cousin Fiona. Or some psycho student either. She knew I was the girl who'd been calling and hanging up.

When Dan got home Martine went ballistic and threatened to walk out and never come back unless he told her the whole truth. So he did. He said I was a high school senior named Amy he met at a video store a few months before they started dating. I came over a few times, we got high, watched movies and fooled around a little. That was it. I was so young he knew it would be immoral to take things any further. Martine asked why he'd lied to her. He said because he was ashamed. Martine asked why I'd been calling recently. He said because I'd broken up with a boyfriend and wanted to hook up with him again. He had told me no, but since I'm a spoiled brat who isn't used to being denied, I turned into a stalker.

I complimented him on his fine lying. He laughed. I said that if I ever ran into Martine on the street I'd be sure to stick to his version of events. He thanked me. I asked if he was truly happy with her and he said yes. I told him that I thought she was incredibly beautiful and sexy. He did not argue. Then I did something evil. I made my voice all soft and sweet and said "Dan, do you know what I really want to do?"

"What?"

"Make love with you. One last time. No strings attached."

There was silence.

He can't resist me.

I'm his heroine.

I whispered "Just call me whenever you want me."

Then I hung up.

Hahahaha!

I know it was whorelike behavior but I felt happy for the first time since he dumped me. Too bad it didn't last. All I want to do right now is crawl back under the covers and not come out till Monday morning.

. . .

I haven't showered since yesterday morning. I smell French! Aaaaggghhh!

Don't read my life. Go live your own!

I don't really want to make love with Dan one last time. I want to marry him. Have his babies. Crazy, I know, but crazy is very now. Being out of your mind is totally in. Rage is all the rage.

I read an *Us* magazine today. I am not sure how old it was but it was all about Britney Spears going insane. With police in her house she locked herself in the bathroom with her baby for three hours. When she came out she was only wearing underpants. Can you imagine a world famous celebrity walking around with her boobs hanging out? Lucky cops! She went completely berserk on them. She kept screaming for her vitamins which is her nickname for her illegal meds. On comment boards everybody was laughing about the incident, trying to predict how long it will be before she kills herself, but as a person who has gone insane I know how tragic this story really is. A true heartbreak. Like the astronaut who drove across the country to get her man back and wore a diaper so she wouldn't have to stop to pee and poo. People mocked her too. I guess the thought of insanity is so scary for some people that they have to laugh it off. But it's not funny at all when you're the person. I would give anything to take back both my drive to Dan's house and my offer to have sex with him again. Where is my pride? Who is there to teach a girl pride?

Sunday, January 20, 2008

I just rocked Joel Seidler's little Jewish world by calling him. Even though when we had dinner I promised him we would be friends again, I knew he didn't believe me, which was smart because I was blatantly lying. But now that I am a crampy, pitiful, lonely half-orphan, I can't be too choosy. We're meeting at a bar with a heated patio where we can smoke ourselves to oblivion. Last one to cough up a tumor is a rotten egg!

LATER: 11:03 p.m.

Having drinks with Joel was either a really healthy thing to do or a really terrible mistake. I can't decide which. I just know I'm in pain. You decide, okay?

As soon as we sat down I told him about my dad's death so I could get all the sympathy out of the way, then I brought up what I really wanted to talk about. I gave him every single detail of my visit to Dan's house and of the phone conversation when I offered him more sex. Joel kept shaking his head like I was a real piece of work.

When I was done he said "I told you to stay away from him but you didn't listen."

When he saw my totally blank face he smiled and said "You didn't just ignore my advice, you forgot it!"

We both laughed and I apologized for being so lame. He asked me if I had called a psychiatrist yet. I told him I definitely would.

Then I said "In the meantime you be my shrink, okay? Tell me what's wrong with me."

I was semi-joking but he didn't notice.

"You won't get defensive?" he asked.

His face was so serious I almost started laughing. I just shook my head. Joel talked for like the next half hour straight. I don't remember all of what he said but the bottom line was that he thinks I am a self-centered borderline-insane nympho. Oh and an incipient alcoholic too. (I didn't know what the word meant either. I just looked it up. It means I am not a drunk yet but soon.) He said the reason I drink so much and have so much stupid sex is to numb my pain. He said I have a lot of sadness inside me but also tons of anger against men. He said that if I don't deal with it I'm going to end up hurting myself or others. He also said I am way too skinny and have major food issues. (What hot gyrl doesn't?) He also said thank god I deferred college because it would have been an unmediated disaster for me to be there right now, especially with my father dying. He thinks I might have ended up jumping off my dorm like he almost did.

The whole time he was listing everything wrong with me I kept arguing with him in my head, thinking of how I was going to defend myself when he stopped. But deep down I knew he was right. I am much more screwed up than I admit. When he was finished I thanked him for being so honest and I promised him I would think about everything he said. He was really impressed with my maturity. Inside I couldn't wait to escape. It all felt so urgent. I just wanted to be alone. Now I am and I wish I weren't. I might even go down the hall and see if my mom is still up.

Monday, January 21, 2008
Martin Luther King's federal birthday was celebrated today but I still had to go to work.

Tuesday, January 22, 2008
I was about to go home for the day when Paul sat me down and told me that there were going to be some changes in the household. Starting Friday, Margaret is going back to work part-time. I pretended to be totally surprised. He said it was a small job redoing some rich dude's media room. She will be working from 10:00 until 2:00 for about a month. This

means we will all have to adjust to meet Cole's needs. Margaret will start pumping and freezing her milk, which will make it possible for me to feed Cole when she's away. Paul said he will make sure to come home for lunch every single day so Cole will only be without both of them from about 9:30 to 12:00. I think this is really intelligent planning. It's going to be hard for Cole to have his mommy gone. He's had boob on demand since the second he was born.

Driving home I heard on the radio Heath Ledger died. Drugs I'm sure. Such a waste. When I got home I crawled into bed and cried over it. Which is weird since I've hardly ever seen any of his movies. I just felt so sorry for his cute girlfriend and their little baby with no daddy. At one point my mom knocked and asked if I was all right. I said "Yes, go away!" I am sure she thought I was crying over my dad. Hey, maybe I was. Hahaha!

Wednesday, January 23, 2008
Long walk with Cole. Freezing but the sky was blue. Cole was so quiet I kept stopping and checking to make sure he wasn't dead. Why is my mind so negative? He was fine, of course, just thinking. Is that possible? To think without words? How about to feel with only words? Possible? Get back to me on that.

. . .

In the afternoon while Margaret was napping, I laid Cole on his floor mat. I sat next to him and watched TV. Cole suddenly decided it was time to flip over onto his stomach for the very first time. He struggled and struggled and then did it. He plopped right over. He was so happy! Such a major achievement! I screamed with joy. Margaret came running down the stairs. She thought he was choking or something but when she saw her baby boy on his stomach, smiling with his hands out at his sides like he was flying, she put her hands on her cheeks and burst out crying. By the end of the day Cole was flipping back and forth, like he'd been doing it his whole life. Wouldn't it be amazing if that happened to grown-ups too? One day, boom, everything turns upside down and you realize that there's so much more to the world than you ever thought?

Friday, January 25, 2008

Margaret started her decorating job today. It was fun to have the house all to myself. It was even more fun knowing that Paul was coming home for lunch. I made sure Cole was fed and napping by the time Paul walked in, so we could eat in peace.

Paul and Dan are brilliant in different ways. Dan mostly knows about film and literature. Paul knows about sports, politics and the stock market. Paul is also way more into current events. Especially the presidential election which we discussed during lunch. Usually I don't like to admit my severe ignorance but since there was no way I could fake it, I told him the truth. I said that I know very little about politics but I want to learn because this is the first election where I actually get to vote. He explained that we are heading toward a huge recession and that the environment is in serious trouble (this I know) and that the war in Iraq has cost us trillions of dollars and our national soul. He likes Obama because he believes nothing is more important than change right now.

"Hillary's not change enough?" I asked.

"Not even close. She's just the male version of her husband."

I thought that was pretty funny.

Sometimes when I am alone with Paul, I can't think of anything interesting to say, so last night, knowing that we were going to be having lunch together, I reread what I blogged about World War One (the stuff Glenn A. Warburg taught me), and today at lunch I regurgitated it. But I did it casually, like it was just one of many historical topics I am an expert on. It impressed the shit out of him.

"I knew I was right to recommend you for admission," he said.

"Even though my transcript sucked."

"No, it didn't. It was just undistinguished."

"Because I didn't apply myself. I hated high school."

"Yeah, you mentioned that during your interview. More than once. I liked your candor."

I gave him the hugest smile. "Well, I knew I was right to defer."

"What do you mean?"

"If I hadn't deferred I wouldn't be sitting here right now with you."

This was the first time I have ever intentionally flirted with him. I couldn't help it. Anyway, he liked it.

When Cole woke up, Paul played with him for a while then helped me change his poopy diaper. Instead of going back to the office, he went upstairs and worked on his computer till Margaret got home. Later at the door Paul handed me my pay envelope. It seemed thicker than usual so when I got to my car I peeked inside. Was there extra cash enclosed? Nope. Something even better. A piece of paper folded around the money. It said:

Dear Miss Kampenfelt:

Since you once expressed a desire to learn some of the bitter truths of human existence that young people in their blind arrogance refuse to consider, here are a few for your reading pleasure. *There are many more, but I don't want to scare you so badly that you panic and attempt a return to the womb.*

10 Bitter Truths

1. Complete honesty is a complete lie.

2. Money is essential to long-term happiness: romantic love is not.

3. Every human being is a paradox. Some hide it better than others.

4. All sex has consequences, most of them dire.

5. Marriage is sacred only to those who have never been married.

6. Never underestimate the tendency of human beings to act contrary to their own best interests.

7. Were it not for the fear of getting caught, most of us would behave like savages.

8. The older you get the faster time moves until months pass like days.

9. There is no such thing as living happily ever after.

10. The world only gets worse.

I have nothing to do tonight (as usual) so I am going to buy some beer and curl up with this shocking list. I will reflect on it and then Monday I will talk it over with Paul. It was so cool of him to take the time to write it for me. My father never did anything this generous and thoughtful. Come to think of it, I don't think anyone else has either. Paul is truly special.

Saturday, January 26, 2008

I was bored this cold winter afternoon so I called Joel Seidler. I was hoping he would have some insightful opinions about the list of bitter truths that I could use for when I talk to Paul. When I was done reading them out loud, Joel asked me where they came from. I told him and he said "Oh, shit. He wants to have sex with you." I told him he was soooooo wrooong! Then he asked me if I had found a good therapist yet and I replied "Oops, call waiting! It's my mom! Talk soon! Bye!"

Barrack Obama kicked major ass in the South Carolina primary election tonight. I watched his whole acceptance speech so I could discuss it Monday with Paul. His main topics are basically hope and change. He makes the future seem amazing. He inspires young people to feel like anything's possible! I so deeply want to believe he's right. I hope nobody murders him before I get a chance to vote.

Sunday, January 27, 2008

I just wrote a fistrate blog about the ten bitter truths and then dleted it by acident. I am a insipid drunk gyrl. A reel non-starter. Not sublime at all. And no way a pardox. I hop no hangover tomorrow!

Monday, January 28, 2008

I've been home from work for ten seconds and I am already writing to you. There is no one else in the whole world I can talk to about this.

Shit. Knock on door. Stand by.

It was my mom, wondering why I ran up the stairs so fast. I told the nosy bitch my bladder was full.

Okay, here goes. Everything was totally normal when I got to work this morning. Margaret was upstairs feeding Cole. Paul was reading his *Wall Street Journal* and sipping his coffee with two sugars and a splash of low-fat milk. At 8:30 I took Cole out for his morning walk. Two minutes later he made the biggest poo ever. I knew because I could smell it even outside in the wind. It's terrible to let a baby sit in his dirty diaper for too long, especially one who has a butthole as sensitive as Cole's, so I turned the stroller around and ran home. As soon as I walked in the back door with Cole, I knew something was wrong. I could just feel it. The silence was tense and massive. Like in a horror movie when the music suddenly stops and you know some seriously scary shit is about to go down. Then I heard yelling upstairs. It was Paul. This shocked me because he is the last person in the world I would expect to yell about anything.

He was saying something like "What? No! I don't expect you to be perfect! That's all in your head! I just expect you to keep your word!"

She yelled back "Jesus Christ! Stop being so dramatic! It's only a couple more hours a day!"

"That's an eternity for a baby!"

"Bullshit! Don't tell me a few extra hours is going to destroy him! Kids are so much more resilient than you think! I am so sick of you telling me how to raise our child!"

"He's not a child! He's an infant! You're his whole universe! And now suddenly he's only going to see you for a few hours in the morning and a few at night and you think that's not going to be traumatic?"

"Only for you. Get out of my way!"

"Don't walk away from me!"

"I'll do as I please! You're not my god damn father!"

"Yeah I know that. Do you?"

"Fuck off!

I heard Margaret walking down the stairs. I grabbed Cole's diaper bag off the counter and ran back outside. I hurried into the garage and laid the diaper mat on the hood of Paul's BMW. I laid Cole on the mat and performed the fastest diaper change in history. What was really lucky and amazing was that he didn't cry at all. I threw away the dirty disgusting diaper then ran outside and strapped Cole back in his stroller. The front door slammed. I saw Margaret walking to her car which was parked out front. I think she was crying. As soon as she drove away I wheeled Cole down the driveway as fast as I could. The back door slammed. I turned my head around and saw Paul walking into the garage. I ran away before he pulled out.

Finishing the walk, all I could think about was that the Spooners have a hidden world I know nothing about. Obviously a lot of the ways that Margaret raises Cole are not her idea at all. They are Paul's. For all I know she hates RIE and hates sharing their bed with the baby. Maybe she doesn't even want to breastfeed him. Maybe she hates being a perfect homemaker too. I have no idea. But it's pretty obvious she is not happy and really misses her decorating work. I don't blame Paul for being pissed. You think you married one person and then they turn out to be somebody else. What a painful shock.

I am remembering Paul's bitter truth #5: *Marriage is sacred only to those who have never been married.*

At lunch Paul returned from work carrying two big salads. We ate them watching *Sports Center* while Cole bounced in his bouncy chair. I knew any minute Paul was going to bring up Margaret and I was right. He looked nervous and said that for the next six weeks or so, instead of working from 10:00 until 2:00 Maggie would be working from 10:00 to 6:00. It turned out this job was a lot more involved than she thought. Paul said he would help out with Cole as much as possible but he would really appreciate it if I could give them an extra couple of hours a day.

"No problem," I replied. "As much as you need."

"Are you sure?"

"Absolutely. I've got no life."

"Thanks so much. I owe you one."

"One what?" I asked all big-eyed and innocent but with a naughty smile.

He wagged a finger at me like "You are so bad."

We both laughed then went back to crunching our salads. We didn't talk much for a while. We just watched the sports highlights. We were both excited and embarrassed at the joke I made. A few minutes later I looked over at him and his beautiful brown eyes looked very sad. I don't think he ever thought his gorgeous dream wife would disappoint him like this. He probably thinks that if she was really happy being a mother and a wife, she wouldn't have agreed to such long hours.

If I was married to a rich awesome man like Paul, I'd stay home barefoot and pregnant and never stop smiling. She is ungrateful.

I think Paul is 100% correct about Cole. A baby can't be with his mother every single minute and then suddenly hardly see her for two months and not have it royally mess up his head. Margaret is Cole's whole universe! He eats from her body! Plus it's hard for a man, no matter how good he is at taking care of babies, to do it alone. They only have so much patience. The fathers, I mean. The babies have pretty much none. That's why for Cole's sake I will give Paul as many hours as he needs.

We did not discuss the ten bitter truths today. He forgot about them and I was too shy to bring them up. Besides, the whole day was one!

Tuesday, January 29, 2008

Why are so many of you writing to me like you're brilliant detectives who have uncovered the most spectacular scandal in the history of mankind? I admit it, okay? I'm infatuated with Paul. There, feel better? Shit, you don't have to be a genius to figure that out. But what does it matter? Why even mention it? I'm not Jade. I don't bone every guy I am attracted to, and I sure as hell don't bone guys who are taken. (Remember, I didn't find out about Martine until it was too late.) But even if I was the kind of girl who slept with married men, no way would Paul do it. I'm 18 and he's 44 and he's my boss.

Margaret got home late today, closer to 7:00 than 6:00. She and Paul were nice to each other but I knew they hadn't recovered from their fight. Their smiles were phony. I acted all chipper like I didn't notice anything was wrong. Before I left, Margaret asked me if I was really going to be okay working so many extra hours. I said absolutely yes, not a problem.

Then I got brave and said "What about you? Are you going to be okay being away from Cole for so long?"

She looked scared for a sec then said "I think so."

I started to get my coat but she stopped me and said "This is an important client, Katie. He's the first person who hired me when I was just starting out. He's sent a ton of work my way. It's the only reason I agreed to it."

The whole thing felt weird. Why was she defending herself to me? I'm just a kid. I smiled really sweetly and said, "Yeah, I figured it was something like that."

Phone ringing. Somebody loves me. Stand by.

Just Joel. He has texted or called me at least 20 times since our talk on Saturday. I never get back to him but he doesn't give up. In his messages he says he is worried about me and just wishes I would let him know I'm alive. That's such bull. He just wants to have another heavy talk. I am blowing him off because I haven't called a psychiatrist yet.

Wednesday, January 30, 2008

Paul hung out with me and Cole today from about 12:00 until 3:00 when he went upstairs to check his email. Except for little interruptions when I had to comfort Cole or change his diaper, we talked pretty much the whole time. We discussed many topics but mostly my favorite one. Me!

You won't believe the risk I took. I told Paul the truth about my recent depression. Crazy, I know. At first I just told him that there was this 26-year-old guy named Dan I used to fool around with every couple of weeks and that he dumped me and it really hurt my feelings. When it was obvious that Paul wasn't judging me at all, I told him Dan's true age (32) and then I slowly added more and more details. When I finally revealed the fact that Dan and I had actually made love, Paul looked really shocked. But before he could say anything, we heard this pretty little sound. We looked over at Cole's basket and saw him laughing for the very first time. (He laughs when he is dreaming but this was the first time awake.) The laughter came out of him almost like hiccups. The most innocent darling sound you've ever heard. Paul was so happy there were tears in his eyes. He is such a sensitive man!

I went back to my story. When I got to the final phone call when I told Dan that he could call me for sex anytime he wanted, Paul shook his head and said "Sweet little suburban Katie. A vixen. Who knew?"

I asked him if vixen meant slut.

He laughed. "I would never call you a slut. The day I'm perfect I'll starting judging other people."

I pretended to be really disappointed. "You mean you're not perfect?"

"Nope, I just look perfect. At least I did until Cole was born. Then I stopped going to the gym."

He slapped his stomach and we both cracked up.

It might be just my imagination but I think after this talk Paul immediately started seeing me differently. I was walking to the fridge to get a Diet Coke and I caught him staring at my ass with a really serious look on his face.

Jade just texted me: *Missin' you, girl!* I wrote back: *Die, ho!*

LATER: 10:38 p.m.

A reader named CohenEliza sent me a pic of two cute little mice having sex on a mousetrap right near the cheese. The bar is pulled back, ready to crush them in two if they move even a millimeter. In the subject line she wrote *You and Paul.* You're pretty funny, CohenEliza. Shame about the slysdexia, though.

Thursday, January 31, 2008

Hahaha! I just woke up and look at this hilarious email I got!

My sweet Katherine, I would like to add something, if I might, to the discussion of you and Mr. Spooner. The following took place in the summer of 1979, when I was twenty years old, vacationing on a nude beach on the Greek isle of Corfu. I was sitting at a taverna one day, sipping a lukewarm Orangina, just about to tuck into my daily dose of moussaka, when I spotted near the shoreline two mongrels humping in the noonday sun. Bravo, I thought, at least someone's getting some tail! After twenty seconds or so, the male reached his climax, but when he turned to run for his life (as intelligent males will), he discovered to his horror that his engorged member was stuck in the bitch's posterior. A frantic tussle ensued, and presto, change-o, the unfortunate lovers were now standing tail-to-tail but still connected! A crowd formed as the male cried out in anguish. The more desperately he tried to free himself, the more profound his agony and the greater the interest of the crowd. This went on for endless minutes until at last the beast's member shrank to a manageable size and he was able to slip free. The crowd cheered and clapped as the poor mutt limped under an awning and licked himself silly. Well, you'll never guess. The very next day at the very same hour, he was at it again. Same beach, same bitch, same result. The idiotic creature had learned nothing from his trial! May Mr. Spooner prove to be more intelligent than that dog. I wish you a painless separation. Your biggest fan, GAHumbert2."

Hilarious, Mr. Humbert from Georgia, but you should not assume that just because Paul and I enjoy each other and I caught him looking at my ass, that we are going to have sex. If I had sex with every man who liked my ass, I would be dead of AIDS.

Saturday, February 2, 2008

Last night Merci Gregoris called and invited me to go out drinking, which surprised me because the last time we spoke she basically called me an embarrassing alcoholic. Since I've been a really good gyrl lately (in case you hadn't noticed), I said okay, even though I hate her.

I met Merci at a loud sports bar that smelled of throw-up. She was sitting on her gigantic ass at a round table with two other silly sorority twats and four ginormous dumb jocks. So that's why I was invited. They were one twat short! I knew if I was going to have any fun with these losers I would have to create it for myself, so I slammed a shot of vodka before I even said hello to them. Then I let them buy me two more.

Pretty soon the whole place was spinning like a merry go round and I had totally forgotten every problem I ever had and would ever have in the future. I got really loud and obnoxious and meanly funny, which no one found hilarious but me. Since I am much smarter than they are, this is not surprising.

Later I escaped and started hunting for a cute boy to kiss. I found one standing alone at the bar, holding a bottle of beer. His name is Nick Dempster and he told me he was 22 but I knew he was lying. I would say 27. He is an inch shorter than me, with longish hair parted in the middle and round glasses. He looks like young John Lennon, with bigger ears and very pretty blue eyes. Almost like a girl's. The next thing I knew he and I were hardcore making out against a wall. Then we were walking down the street holding hands. Then we were in my Volvo and he was driving. Then we were back at his little apartment having sex. These are like separate scenes from a movie. I have no idea what connected them. Which is weird. I wonder if he put something in my cocktail because usually when I drink I remember everything or nothing. This was somewhere in between.

Anyway, right in the middle of the sex I started thinking about Rory. I almost never think about him. Suddenly I felt terrible that I cheated on him. I started crying into the pillow. And then I started thinking about Dan and how I would never kiss him again and I started crying even harder. It was almost like I wanted to feel as bad as I could! What was pretty disgusting is that Nick Dempster never stopped pumping me the whole time I was bawling. When he finally finished I barely noticed, because I was too busy thanking god that I haven't done anything sexual with Paul. I knew right then that I never will. It would be inexcusable.

I woke up this morning with a brain tumor headache. I opened one eye and looked around. One of the walls had an ugly abstract painting hanging on it. There was a bong tipped over on the dresser. Through the window I could see an icicle drip drip dripping in the painful sun. I rolled over and saw Nick waking up. He ran a hand through his hippie hair.

"What do you know?" he said, smiling at me. "No pterodactyl syndrome."

"What's that?"

"Well, you know what a pterodactyl is, don't you?"

"Some sort of machine?"

"A giant dinosaur bird with wings fifty feet across and giant teeth."

"Okay."

"The pterodactyl syndrome is when I have sex with a girl for the first time and the next morning I wish a pterodactyl would come crashing through the window, grab her with its big feet and drop her in the lake somewhere."

"This happens a lot?"

"Yeah. But not with you. The last time it didn't happen, I ended up dating the girl for almost a year."

"Lucky her."

I was being sarcastic. He didn't notice. He got up to pee and I watched him walk to the bathroom. His butt was okay but he had love handles. Definitely 27. I thought about the night before and this is when I first wondered if Nick had slipped something into my drink. For breakfast he made us milk shakes with banana and honey which he said had potassium and glucose to make hangovers vanish. I drank it in about three huge gulps then chained three cigarettes. Keep smoke alive! My hangover did not go away.

At the door he started kissing me with his banana breath and telling me how gorgeous I was. If I could have puked into his mouth I would have. I couldn't believe how much I hated him. Walking to my car I looked up at the dead white sky and wished there was a pterodactyl up there to carry me away.

. . .

I've felt sick and sore all day. Why didn't I just drive home once I knew there was no way I was going to have fun? I should have just curled up and read a book. I am still only on page 13 of *Who Was Changed and Who Was Dead*. Did I really think getting wasted and boning a stranger was going to make my life better?

Right now Mark Aubichon and my mom are sitting around the kitchen table planning their wedding and laughing their happy asses off. I hear them down there. What could be more depressing?

I wish I had never given Nick Dempster my phone number. I am almost positive he slipped something in my drink.

LATER: 9:18 p.m.
Nothing to do tonight so I stayed home and regretted.

Your emails today have been full of hate, judgment, crude humor, accusations and insults. I know this is the price I pay for being honest. Still it's hard to take. From now on I will delete all emails the second they turn cruel.

Just so you understand that I am not a total waste of space, I did something very cool recently. I wasn't going to blog about it because I was afraid if I told you when and where I did this thing, you would figure out what state I live in. But I will leave out all specifics. What I did was volunteer for Barack Obama! (I have misspelled his first name many times and not one of you corrected me. Dummies!) I woke up at 5:00 a.m. and drove really far to the place where the speech was going to be. My job was to show people to their seats. My reward for doing this was that I got to hear him speak in person close-up. When he finally arrived and the crowd began screaming, stomping on the bleachers and clapping their hands to "Yes, We Can!" my whole body shook with excitement. I trembled along with the sea of inspired people. When he finally walked across the stage I was like a deranged groupie. I started screaming and reaching out my arms to him like he was my savior. He is skinny but really gorgeous. He made a touching, awesome speech. On the news I was in front of the flag behind him and to the left. Sorry I can't tell you which speech it was or which news. Paul was amazing to let me go do this. He was proud of my service, he said. He even paid me for the hours I missed!

Sunday, February 3, 2008

Nick Dempster left a romantic message today like we are boyfriend and girlfriend. Only thing is, he got my name wrong. What a spectacular douche. I will not call him back.

Super Tuesday, February 5, 2008

Obama did awesome tonight in the biggest day of elections ever. He didn't beat the crap out of Hillary, but he tied her and for an unknown black man that's pretty huge. The only tragic and embarrassing thing was that I didn't vote! You're going to want to strangle me at how stupid I am but no one told me I had to register first! I went down to the school all proud and excited to vote for the first time and I was totally humiliated.

I yelled at my mom "Why didn't you tell me I had to register before I could vote?!"

She said "Sweetie, it never occurred to me. You've never shown the slightest interest in politics."

I said "I'm not interested in politics! I'm interested in Barack Obama!"

Wednesday, February 6, 2008

Joel Seidler texted me at work today, begging me to have dinner with him. I should have just said no. It was a horrible, painful night. I feel like crawling under my duvet and sleeping forever. It started off okay. I told him everything that happened since the last time we talked. Even though I knew it was pretty cruel, I told him about Nick Dempster. I did it for two reasons. One is that when you tell a male friend about slutty sex with another guy it's a way of telling him that you would never ever have sex with him. (If Joel and I are going to be real friends he must know this.) The second is that I thought maybe he would say something to make me feel better. Like "Hey, don't beat yourself up over it. Every girl has stranger-sex at least once in their lives." That sort of thing.

Instead he thought for a long time, staring darkly and blowing smoke, then said "Were you sexually abused when you were little?"

WTF? Not what I'd expected! I laughed. Sort of. More like a snort. I was thinking "Dude, what planet are you from? Get over your Jewish self." I personally know nine girls in my high school class who have either been molested, date-raped, raped or incested. And I have always been really thrilled not to be one of them. Whenever I see grown-up versions of them on TV crying over what happened to them 20 years ago, I'm always like "Yeah, it sucked. Men are shit. I get it. Time to move on, babe." Joel just assumed from my snorting reaction that my answer to his question was "Hell no," so he flicked his cigarette and started to think harder, like maybe there was some other reason why I'm such a crazy bitch.

While he was thinking, I started remembering some really disturbing stuff that occurred when I was little. It's not like its stuff I forgot about. I just never thought it was very important. It was like a dirty story you heard that happened to somebody else. Or memories of an R-rated movie you saw by accident one night on TV when you were too little to understand it. Or something you fantasized about when you were stoned and the next day you aren't sure if you imagined it or if it really happened. (Does this even make sense?) Anyway, while Joel was thinking, I realized these memories weren't some cool secret. They were serious. Then the question was, Do I tell Joel or continue to keep it private? I think maybe he saw this question on my face, because he started saying "What? What? What?"

So I told him what happened. Every summer when I was little we used to rent a cabin on a lake. Our next door neighbor was named Mr. Silaggi. He was a chubby Hungarian man with a squashed button nose like Santa Claus and a thick accent. He used to sit around all day in his bathing suit and black knee socks. The summer before my parents got divorced my dad quit drinking and hid our TV in the garage. He wanted no distractions because he was going to write a book about the worst injuries in sports history. My mom had just lost my baby sister (she was born dead, two months premature). She was so depressed, she didn't really care about no TV. But I did. A lot.

Whenever I got bored, which was almost every day because there were no other kids around, my mom sent me next door to watch TV with Mr. Silaggi. Mrs. Silaggi would serve us lemonade and little folded-over Hungarian cookies with prunes inside. Whenever Mrs. Silaggi left the house, Mr. Silaggi would put me on his lap and stick his hand in my bathing suit bottom. He would rub me and squirm around underneath. I didn't really know what he was doing but I knew that even though it felt weird and good, it was not allowed and if I told my mom about it, she would never let me watch TV over there again. So I didn't tell her or anyone else.

The next summer the divorce had started so my dad didn't come with us to the lake. The first thing my mom did when we got there was get the TV out of the garage and screw the cable back in. There was no reason for me to hang out with Mr. Silaggi anymore. I remember being happy about that but scared he might be mad at me. The last time I went over there was one day when my mom asked the Silaggis to babysit. The second Mrs. Silaggi left the room, Mr. Silaggi pulled me up onto his lap. But this time when he put his hand inside my bathing suit I slapped him. Just hard enough to make him stop. When my mom got back, I told her I didn't want to see Mr. Silaggi anymore. She asked why and I said that he had gotten mad at me for spilling my lemonade and spanked me. This freaked her out and I never had to go over there again.

For the rest of the summer whenever we walked past Mr. Silaggi's house and he was outside hosing down his flowers or whatever, he would stare at me like he wanted to kill me.

Thinking about it now, maybe he was just afraid I was going to tell someone. I don't know. I remember wanting to tell my mom everything but thinking that she either wouldn't believe me or she'd think it was all my fault.

When I finished the story, Joel had tears in his eyes. He said "Please get into therapy. I think you're going to discover that what happened with Mr. Silaggi has had a huge affect on you."

"What do you mean?"

"I mean it's affected you in ways you can't even imagine."

I started to argue with him but he said that if he was right then I really have no idea what I'm talking about, because, as he said, the affect is in ways I cannot imagine.

Joel drove me home. I kissed him on the cheek and jumped out. At the front door I turned around and waved, smiling like an idiot. Chipper, spunky Katie! He waved back and drove away. For some reason I didn't go inside. I stood there, looking all around me. The whole dark world seemed cold and scary all of the sudden. I felt this terrible fear that Joel was right and that what happened to me was a way bigger deal than I thought. My heart started pounding really hard. It was like I thought Mr. Silaggi was going to jump out of the bushes any second and stab me to death. I thought maybe the sight of the moon would make me feel better, but I looked everywhere and there wasn't one.

. . .

Nick Dempster just left another message. He can't believe I won't call him back. Mr. Cutie isn't used to being blown off.

Thursday, February 7, 2008

A lot of you girls who have been sexually abused or raped have been writing to me in the past 24 hours. You feel bad for me and want to know how I am feeling. How I am feeling is really shaky. Many of you also think I am highly fortunate to have a friend like Joel and I agree with you. Our talks are painful but I always grow from them.

After dinner I was lying in bed thinking about this weird phase I went through in third grade where I refused to take baths or wash my hair and sometimes to gross boys out, I would eat flies, ants and daddy longleg spiders. My mother said if I didn't stop it she was going to take me to a child psychiatrist so I stopped. Now I am wondering why I wanted to treat myself so badly. I was using my body like a garbage can. Am I still doing it today? For instance, I let Nick Dempster have sex with me just because he wanted to. Why? I was sobbing into the pillow for fuck's sake and he didn't stop! What a terrible person he is! And what about Dan? Did we really make love or did he just molest me? I don't really know the answers anymore.

. . .

All day Paul kept asking me what was wrong and I kept saying "Nothing, I am just tired." There is no way I want to
discuss this with him.

Some ugly freak on YouTube is claiming that ten years ago
he gave Barack Obama a blow job in a limo while they did
cocaine together. Everybody knows it's a lie but meanwhile
the video has gotten thousands of hits. I hope it doesn't
destroy him. It's times like these when I really hate the
world. It would be so great to be able to believe in just one
good pure perfect thing. That's all I want.

Friday, February 8, 2008

This morning I told my mom I would like to start therapy.
She calmly sipped her coffee and asked why. I said that there
were some issues concerning my dad I wanted to deal with.
She said that sounded like a wonderful idea. Deep down I
knew she was celebrating. How do I know? Because right in
the middle of lunch while I was laughing my ass off at Paul's
imitation of Margaret's decorating client (he is gay, rich and
from Texas), she called to tell me that I have an appointment
tomorrow with Dr. Elaine Sherman. Mama didn't waste no
time! Hahaha!

   When I hung up, Paul asked what that was all about. I
lied and said my mom had made me a gyno appointment so

I can go back on the pill. He asked why I was doing that since I don't have a boyfriend.

I said "I'll get one soon. I have to. If I go too long without sex I turn into a werewolf."

You should have seen his shocked face. I deserve to have my ass kicked for remarks like these. Haha! But isn't it amazing how fast I thought of that perfect lie? I am so creative.

Even though I am never going to have sex with Paul, that does not mean I am not dying of curiosity to know whether he wants to or not. If I learned that he was secretly fiending over my body I would be incredibly flattered. Margaret is so lucky to have him, she has no idea. Lately when she comes home from work she's in a really great mood, still high from her exciting day, but when she sees Paul everything changes. She turns grumpy and serious. She doesn't even kiss him hello. And when Paul kisses her she barely reacts. What happened? They were so happy once. Maybe the brawl I overheard was just one of many. Paul never mentions any problems in their marriage. Is he just being a gentleman?

Saturday, February 9, 2008
I am happy that Dr. Sherman is a female, because the last thing I want to be thinking about while I'm bearing my soul is whether my shrink is sprouting a boner. I like her a lot.

She is the fun, cool, warm Jewish mom everybody wishes they had. Great big toothy smile. Black poodle hair parted down the middle. Big hips. Black boots and shawl covering big, probably saggy boobs. Behind her desk is a framed photo of her with her handsome bearded husband and three smiling boys. My mom made an excellent choice.

Instead of gushing my whole life the first day, I just discussed what brought me there. She listened to the Mr. Silaggi story, taking notes and asking simple questions. When I was done she inquired about my feelings toward men in general. "Men with a capital M," she said. I told her that I prefer brilliant older ones because they know who they are and I can learn from them. I told her I find guys my own age shallow, insecure and intellectually unstimulating. Plus they come way too fast! She laughed at this. Which made me think we can be friends.

Then I guess because I had brought up sex, she asked me the weirdest question. She asked if my nipples were sensitive. Why did she ask this? It sort of freaked me out for a sec. Do girls who have been molested have sensitive nipples or something? Insensitive ones? Mine are on the numbish side. When guys suck on them, I pretend it's driving me crazy but it doesn't. I told her this and she scribbled it down on her yellow pad.

When our time was over, she said "I have homework for you. I want you to write a letter to Mr. Silaggi."

"I'm pretty sure he's dead."

"It's not for him. It's for you. I want you to get your thoughts and feelings down on paper. Write anything you want. Just make sure it's the truth."

I agreed.

I got an email from VaudevireLM, who asked me why I don't go on the birth control pill for real instead of lying about it. Well, Vaud, the reason is simple: I am too vain. I break out from the pill. Mostly on my forehead. Also I get 25% less horny. Plus pulling out and condoms work great. The hard part is being strong enough to demand one or the other. For instance, I was so messed up, I never told Nick Dempster to do either. He wore a condom anyway, I think.

Sunday, February 10, 2008
Obama kicked more mother-butt this weekend in Maine and somewhere else. I saw a little bit of a speech. He said he wants kids to go to school not just to learn how to pass tests but also to learn music, art and poetry. How unbelievable is that? I bet my old boss Glenn A. Warburg loves him too. If I ever speak to him again, I am going to impress him with how much I know about politics.

Monday, February 11, 2008

Today while we were eating naughty take-out burgers, Paul mentioned that Cole has been having nightmares lately. He starts crying in his sleep but even after they wake him up he goes on weeping for like half an hour. Margaret thinks they are just the normal "night terrors" that all kids have but Paul thinks it's because he is traumatized from Margaret being gone all the time. He said that when he shared this theory she went ballistic.

"What are you going to do?" I asked.

"What can I do?" he replied. "Love my kid and hope Maggie decides to be a mother again someday."

He is really pissed at her and I don't blame him. If she wanted a career so bad she shouldn't have had children.

Tuesday, February 12, 2008

Three more wins for Obama. Yes, we can! Yes, we can! Yes, I can!

Wednesday, February 13, 2008

I cried all the way home from work. My hormones are back. Which means I am not pregnant. Yeehaw!

Thursday, February 14, 2008

My first Valentine's Day ever that I did not have a boy-friend. The last thing I expected was that Paul would give me a present. When he handed me the little box, my first thought was that it was going to be some sort of gag gift. Come on, he's a married man! Well, it wasn't. It was a rose-gold antique locket with three tiny diamonds and a ruby in it. By far the most beautiful thing I've ever owned. I was so surprised I couldn't even speak. He said to open it. I did and inside the locket was a tiny picture of Cole.

"Someday when you have a child of your own, you can put his picture in there but for now Cole will have to do."

I threw my arms around his neck and gave him the biggest hug ever. It wasn't enough. I just had to give him a kiss. But I knew if I kissed him with too much passion and he freaked out, it would be the most embarrassing moment of my life. So I kissed him half on the mouth and half on the cheek. He was definitely not expecting it but he didn't mind. So I did it again and then sort of paused near his face. His breathing changed. When he gently pushed me away, he said "You probably shouldn't tell Maggie about this." I didn't know if he meant the locket or the kisses. I still don't know. Maybe both.

. . .

Please don't tell me that kissing Paul was wrong. Trust me, I know. But sometimes when a gyrl is hormonal and lonely, life happens, okay? Deal with it.

Once my period comes I will stop being insane, I promise. Don't worry, I will not try to seduce him. And do you know why? Bitter truth #4: *All sex has consequences, most of them dire*. You see? Paul is a good teacher and I am a good student.

I would kill for a beer right now but Mark is getting annoyed with me for constantly stealing his supply. He calls me "Miss Beer Belly" now. He thinks this nasty nickname will get me to stop drinking because he knows I would rather die than be fat. Only problem is I have lost weight lately! My stomach looks the best it ever has!

The liquor store that takes my fake I.D. is 20 minutes away. Driving there would require the putting on of clothes. Maybe it's worth it. Besides beer, I would also like some dark chocolate, potato chips and a big box of Sweet Tarts. How come? You guessed it. Hormones, baby!

On TV the newscaster is talking about a psycho kid who went berserk on a college campus today and started shooting people. There have been so many incidents like this lately. Sometimes it feels like there are thousands of sick people out there ready to attack. That's why we need to live life to the fullest while we are here because it could all be over so quickly. One minute you're trying to discover your bliss and the next you've got a bullet in your brain.

Friday, February 15, 2008

This is when most bloggers would start lying big-time, but no matter how hard it is to tell you this, and no matter how much you'll hate me for it, I refuse to bullshit you. I know what you are thinking. Bitter truth #1: *Complete honesty is a complete lie*. Well, maybe Paul's wrong about that one.

This morning I thought if I never tongue-kissed Paul in my entire life I would look back one day and think "Shit, why didn't I do it just once?" Yes, all sex has dire consequences but is kissing sex? Not really. Only if you let it be.

As soon as Paul got home for lunch all I could think about was when and how I would kiss him. Since it was only going to happen once, it had to be perfect. I got a little bit obsessed. Like when you're dead broke and you're all out of cigarettes and you're walking down the street and all you can think about is bumming one but no one you see is smoking and pretty soon you get so desperate you will smoke anything. You turn into an animal. You start looking in the gutter for a butt. That's what I was like.

The perfect moment did not come during lunch. We ate big salads and played with Cole and talked about a million things. Then afterwards, Paul went straight upstairs to work. I was so frustrated I felt like screaming "No, no, come back! I have some dessert for you!" After Cole went down for his second nap, I walked all the way to Paul's office door. I lifted my fist to knock but chickened out.

By the time Margaret got home from work, Paul was in the kitchen cooking a pot of his world-famous chili and I was so nervous I could hardly talk anymore. As usual she greeted me and asked about my day, but barely even said hello to her husband. She loaded the day's pumped milk from her little portable cooler into the freezer then took Cole upstairs to nurse.

Paul had my pay envelope ready. He handed it to me and said "Goodbye, sweet girl, have a great weekend." All of the sudden the moment was perfect. I could barely breathe. I put both my hands around his neck (they were shaking!), and I smiled sort of crooked and cute and said "I still haven't officially thanked you for the present." I gave him the sexiest, slowest, deepest, wettest kiss. I honestly thought he was going to die he grabbed me so tightly.

"You're incredible," he whispered painfully.

Almost every guy I've ever kissed in my life says something about my beauty within ten seconds after they kiss me for the first time, but nothing was as wonderful as hearing it from Paul.

"So are you," I whispered back.

I popped up on tiptoe, kissed him deeply again, then spun around and walked quickly to the door. I grabbed my coat and left without saying anything.

Before you write me a vicious email, ask yourself if deep down you aren't a teensy bit jealous?

Paul paid me $950. When I got home, I did the math. 40 hours at the usual rate of $13 per hour comes out to $520. 22 hours of overtime at the overtime rate of $15 an hour comes out to $330. So he paid me exactly $100 extra. Was this an accident or a Valentine's Day tip? Maybe if he had known the kiss was coming, he would have given me $200 extra! Hahaha!

LATER: 11:58 p.m.
Bleeding has begun. Perfect timing. Seriously.

Saturday, February 16, 2008
I went to therapy today totally planning to tell Dr. Elaine Sherman what happened with Paul and I. But I just couldn't.

I knew what she would say. I told her about Dan instead. She pretended it wasn't that big a deal but I could tell she was pretty shocked by his age. She asked me a ton of questions about what our sex life was like. I'm not sure what she was getting at. She never lets me know what she's thinking. Toward the end of the hour she asked if I had any new insights into Mr. Silaggi. I was too embarrassed to tell her that I hadn't thought about him at all since our last appointment, so I shared an old insight instead. The one about me eating ants and daddy longlegs and how this showed a lack of self-esteem on my part that might be related to what Mr. Silaggi did to me. She agreed completely. Then she asked if I had written the letter to him yet. I lied and said that I was almost finished.

I don't really want to be in therapy right now. I am not comfortable discussing Paul with Dr. Sherman.

Genius idea. Stand by.

Okay I just sent an email from my mom's old gmail account. Check it out:

Dear Dr. Sherman:
First off, I want to thank you for making time in your busy schedule to see Katie. She really is something, isn't she? One of a kind, all right. As much as she is enjoying your sessions

together, I have decided, because of her recent major weight loss,
that it might be a better idea if I send her to a psychiatrist who
specializes in young women and their many food/body issues. A
national epidemic! Thank you so much for your time.
Yours truly, Caroline Kampenfelt
P.S. Please send me your bill for the first two sessions and I will
pay it asap.

Maybe I am a coward for stopping therapy but I honestly
think it would be disloyal and inappropriate to discuss me
and Paul's relationship with anybody else. Except you, of
course!

Sunday, February 17, 2008
Nick Dempster just called again. I am so sad and lonely
I almost picked up. Boy, he must have really loved date-
raping me.

Dr. Sherman wrote right back to my mom at the old gmail
address and said no problem, she understood perfectly. She
said I was a special girl whom it was a pleasure to get to
know even if only for such a short period of time.

I am free! My mom will never suspect a thing until she realizes that she got a bill for two sessions but never received
another one, and by then who cares?

Monday, February 18, 2008

Today while Paul worked upstairs, I took Cole for a long walk, fed him, and changed a diaper that was so overflowing I had to hose him down in the tub. Later Paul went out and brought us back sushi which I usually don't like (Rory calls it mermaid clits) but it tasted much better eating it with Paul who at least knew what everything was. I kept thinking we were going to kiss again any minute but we didn't. Paul acted like it had never happened. In a way it hurt but the other half of me knew that he was right.

While he cleared away the containers I went upstairs and put Cole down for his second nap. Paul likes me to sit next to his crib singing and stuff until he is sound asleep, which I usually don't mind. But today it was killing me because I wanted to be downstairs so badly. Anyway, Cole conked out pretty fast. After I held a pillow over his face. (Kidding!) Then I grabbed the baby monitor and ran back to Paul who was sitting in the den watching sports highlights. My dad hated it whenever I talked during *Sports Center* so I didn't say a word. I just sat down next to him and flipped through a magazine.

When a commercial came on Paul said "Why are you so quiet?"

I replied "I don't want to annoy you."

"Impossible."

And before I could say anything he grabbed my hand, pulled me onto his lap and started kissing me. I was so shocked I started laughing. But then I stopped pretty fast because his hand went up my shirt. I can't even describe what happened in detail. If I do I'll have to change my underwear. Haha! When he started to unzip my jeans I said "I'm having my period." And he said "So what?" That turned me on. I loved that he wanted me so badly. There is no way I would have stopped him but then Cole started crying in the baby monitor. We stopped, all sweaty and breathing hard. I climbed off his lap and ran away. Honestly? I was glad Cole woke up. I don't really like sex during my period. Taking out the tampon kills the mood.

I rocked Cole and sang to him and by the time he fell back asleep Paul had returned to his computer. I cleaned up the kitchen and watched TV and I didn't see him again until Margaret got home at 6:15. She seemed weirdly quiet. I got this terrible fear that Paul had already told her about us. Or else she just suspected it. I asked her if she was okay.

She breathed out and said "My client's just being a pain in the butt is all. He keeps changing his mind."

Later when Paul walked me to the door he whispered "To stop like that was a crime against nature, wasn't it?"

"Totally," I whispered back.

Actually I was thinking just the opposite, that if we hadn't stopped, that would have been the crime. Hello? I believe it's called adultery!

Tuesday, February 19, 2008

A wonderful day with Paul. We talked and kissed and touched each other but did not make love. If we keep things like this it will be perfect.

It's snowing like a bitch right now and I am cozy with two beers and a half-full pack of Kent Lights. The election is playing on TV. I can't believe how much I love politics now. Obama is kicking more cellulite-ass tonight, winning his tenth primary in a row. One expert just said to put a fork in Hillary because she's done. And this bald guy replied "Maybe not a fork. But a spoon." If you imagine putting a spoon inside Hillary Clinton, you could puke for an hour. I know I'm super harsh toward Hillary but she reminds me way too much of my mom, and my mom being president is my worst nightmare.

Paul told me something hilarious today. He donated the maximum legal amount of $2,300 to Obama. A few days later Margaret asked him to go online and give the same amount to Hillary. He said "Sure thing, honey." But he never did it! How funny is that? How cool is it that we both love Obama? How rhetorical am I? Hahaha! I am in such a good mood!

LATER: 2:18 a.m.

As I was about to turn out the lights and go to sleep, I heard a car door slam. I looked out the window and saw Rory practically running to my front door. I knew he must have finally found out about my dad dying or he would never come over like this against my wishes. I also knew he'd have some weed with him. I was right about both. He said he felt terrible about my dad and was really hurt I didn't tell him at least in an email. I told him thanks for feeling terrible but we all knew he was going to die any minute so it wasn't that big a deal.

Rory was so nervous being alone with me that his hands trembled as he rolled the joint. He apologized again for everything he did to me, not just boning Jade but for all of the times he got crazy-jealous and physically abused me and accused me of shit I didn't do. He really made me laugh when he told me how bad Jade was in bed. He said she got all squirmy and psychotic. She bit his shoulders and chest really hard and clawed his back. And guess what else? The rumor is true! She's smelly down there! I almost peed myself laughing, imagining her like some crazy stinky freak biting and shredding his sensitive freckly skin. And yet he boned her anyway. Many, many times. Guys are weak.

This is going to sound certifiably insane but I fell a little bit back in love with Rory tonight. Almost the way I felt the first few weeks after we met. I couldn't help it. He was being so kind and sympathetic and sweet. And I was stoned! The next thing I knew we were making love. I think I thought if I did this I would be less likely to have sex with Paul. Maybe it's true.

The best part was lying there afterwards and listening to him tell me how much he loved me and how beautiful I am. I was like Narcissus gazing at myself in the swimming pool. Huh? I mean pool of water! I am still a little bit high. Hee-heehee. Don't worry I didn't drown in the deep end. I slept for like an hour in his arms and when I woke up and realized what I had done, I looked out the window and since there weren't any pterodactyls around, I got up and kicked his ass out. I sure hope he doesn't think it will ever happen again.

Good night, moon!

Wednesday, February 20, 2008

This morning I told Paul I'm feeling guilty and scared at how close we are to making love. He said he feels the same way. We agreed that we should do everything but. This made me feel so much better. I started laughing I was so happy. The whole day, every second we were alone all we did was kiss and touch and then kiss some more. At one point he pulled down my jeans, kneeled down on the floor and started gently kissing my ass. It was the sexiest, most exciting thing ever.

Joel just texted me for like the fifth time in three days. I haven't called him back because I know if I do I will tell him the truth about me and Paul.

Jade left a message, too. I guess she heard that Rory and I hung out and now she wants to tell me how he practically raped her and how she was too scared to dump him. I texted her back: *Sorry about the deadly yeast. Get well soon.* I never did anything to deserve the way she treated me.

Thursday, February 21, 2008

I gave Paul a blow job today. First time. It was amazing. I have never been this attracted to anyone. Even more than to Dan. And that's saying a lot. Maybe that's why I'm so scared of making love with him.

When Margaret got home from work Paul was out buying food for dinner. As she was taking off her coat she froze and stared at me. For a second I thought there was cum hanging off my nose or something.

"What?" I said.

"I want to ask you something."

"Okay."

"Since I started working full-time—"

"Yeah?"

"Have you noticed a change?"

"What do you mean?"

"In Cole."

I burst out laughing. "No, no, no. He's fine."

"Are you sure?"

"Positive. I mean, the first week, he definitely cried a little bit more than usual. And maybe he was a little more needy. But he's great now. Just look at him. See how happy he is?"

Margaret walked over to his bouncy chair. Cole was kicking and kicking with a big smile. She unstrapped his seat belt and lifted him out. She kissed him all over and made him giggle. She got tears in her eyes. Boy, did I feel guilty.

Friday, February 22, 2008

Stop writing to tell me what a disgusting person I am. I try not to read your vicious letters but sometimes I can't resist and then I feel worse about myself than I already do. If you don't stop, I will shut down the contact button and none of you will ever be able to write to me again.

. . .

Cole is obsessed with the TV remote control. Margaret says to keep it away from him because it's the dirtiest thing in the house. No it's not, lady. Not anymore.

Sunday, February 24, 2008

Something is wrong with me. Yesterday afternoon I was lying in bed missing Paul when the phone rang. I saw Dan's name and I knew the only smart thing to do was not pick up and not even listen to the voice mail he left. Delete and move on. Forget he ever happened. But what did I do instead? I answered and acted all happy to hear from him.

"Hey, stranger! What's goin' on?"

"Oh, not much. Working hard. How about you?"

I could tell from his voice that he had decided to accept my sex offer. I knew it. But I had made the offer before I fell in love with Paul who is much kinder to me than Dan. He is also sexier and more mature. Paul has ruined me! No other man compares! So what did I do when Dan asked if I wanted to come over and watch a movie?

I said "Cool! What time?"

I am such an idiot. Why did I do it? I knew what would happen. Something is seriously wrong with me.

Anyway I did it. I went over to his house and had sex with him. No condom. Afterwards lying on the sticky couch with a framed picture of Martine staring at me from the mantle I realized that I had just been used. He didn't love me. He just wanted a beautiful young body to orgasm in. Which is what I let him do. So I decided to get back at him. I pretended I needed some advice, but I really just wanted to crush his ego. I told him all about Paul. When I got to the part where Paul and I kissed for the first time, I could tell Dan was getting angry but trying to control it. He didn't lose his shit until I got to the blow job.

He jumped up and shouted "What're you doing?! The guy's a piece of shit!"

"What does that make you?"

"I'm fourteen years older than you not twenty-six years! And I'm not married! And I'm not your fuckin' boss! You know it's a federal offense, right? To screw your employee?"

I acted all casual and amused. "Will you chill out? We haven't had sex. Wow, I had no idea you were the jealous type."

"Oh, please. I was never jealous about Cory, was I?"

"Rory."

"What happened to him?"

"We broke up."

"Well get back together. Or find someone else your own age. But stay away from this Spooner guy. He's a dirtbag."

I started to cry. I don't know why. He kneeled down and handed me my shirt and said "Look, I know you've been through a hard time lately, what with your dad dying and everything but sleeping with a married man is only going to make you feel worse. You need to get into therapy, Katie. Serious therapy."

"I already am."

He was surprised.

"Did you tell him about Spooner?"

"It's a female. No, not yet. Only about you."

"Great. Well, tell her I made it clear to you tonight that I don't ever want to see you again. What happened between us was wrong. All of it from the beginning. I saw you tonight because I was weak but it won't happen again. I'm sorry to say this so soon after—"

"You fucked me?"

"Your father died." He handed me the rest of my clothes. "Go home now. One of us has to be strong. I'm the adult, so it's going to be me."

I don't get mad very often but when I do it's scary. I got dressed really slowly and did not say a word. Then I walked to the fridge and took out an open bottle of white wine. I popped the cork and said "By the way, I lied. I'm not on the pill." Then I walked out the door, laughing and swigging the wine. On the way to the car I wondered if he was watching me, but I did not even turn around to find out. I just drove away.

. . .

If Dad is so jealous over what happened with Paul that he doesn't want to see me anymore then he can die as far as I'm concerned. Paul is a better person anyway. I just wish I hadn't gone over there. I feel like I cheated on Paul. I know that's stupid but it's how I feel.

The Oscars are on right now. I don't care who wins. I missed every good Hollywood movie this year. Both of them. Ha! Thank god I have work tomorrow. Paul will kiss me out of my misery.

Monday, February 25, 2008

I could build up what happened today into some huge, amazing romantic story but it wasn't like that at all. There was no orchestra playing or thunder clapping or waves crashing. What happened was intensely real. If they made a movie of it there would be no music, just the sound of our breaths and a branch tapping the window and Cole snoring gently in his bouncy chair.

Paul makes love different than Dan. Dan acts like he's loving it more than anything in the world but at the same time wants it over with as soon as possible. Paul is slow and tender like he never wants it to end. I believe this is true love-making.

. . .

Paul definitely loves me. No, not in the way he loves Margaret and Cole but not just in the way you love a friend either. I think he respects me and laughs with me and lusts for me and enjoys teaching me and when you put all this together it's a wonderful special kind of love. We did it three times today. Twice during Cole's nap and once we just turned Cole's chair around and made sure we were very quiet, because Paul says kids are biologically programmed to absorb everything.

Three times is pretty amazing for a man Paul's age. He said he hadn't done it that many times in one day since college.

"Not even with Margaret when you first met?"

"Are you kidding? At very best it was three times a week. These days it's three times a month if I'm lucky."

"Poor boy."

"Tell me about it."

I am afraid to keep describing what today was like. I don't want to make it seem like less than it was.

All day we held hands nonstop even when we were eating. I would give anything to spend a whole night with him. Maybe he can pretend to go away on a business trip and we can get a motel room in the city. I bet we would hold hands all night, even while we were sleeping.

Tuesday, February 26, 2008

The first email I opened today was from an Arabic fundamentalist who said if I lived in his country I would be killed for "crimes against chastity." I wrote back and said that as benighted as his country is, I didn't really believe they would kill a girl my age just for falling in love. And he wrote back that a few years ago they hung a 16-year-old girl for way less than what I did with Paul. I wrote back and said "Well, then thank god I live in America and please don't ever write to me again." I feel like calling the FBI and asking them to track this guy down and open up a can of Guantanomo on his ass. Hahaha! Suddenly I'm all right wing!

Must run. Can't be late for work. Can you believe I actually get paid to spend time with the man I love?

Wednesday, February 27, 2008

Paul had meetings all day. Cole was a fucking nightmare. It was not his fault. He's been drooling and sucking on his hand and these are the sure signs of teething. I gave him some herbal drops and that helped a little. Finally Paul got home but we had barely any time together before Margaret got back early. Good thing she called first and warned us. I guess this means she doesn't suspect anything or she would never have called. If she was not so self-involved with her career she would definitely sense something weird was going on because lately I turn into such a chatterbox the second she walks in. Paul is pretty much calm, except every now and then the tips of his ears turn dark red. (Paul is a physically beautiful man. His only tiny flaw is that he needs to shave between his eyebrows. If we were a real couple I would tell him.)

Margaret was worried about how tired Cole looked. I explained that he has begun teething so he only took one nap and it was only for 40 minutes. She looked at me like it was my fault. Hey, lady, if you don't like the job I'm doing then quit your stupid career and start acting like a mother! Actually, no, I take that back. I hope her job lasts forever.

I am in an extra foul mood right now. When I got home there were all these cruel emails waiting for me. I deleted most of them based on the subject line. And then I saw one from Joel Seidler and I thought "Hey, good old Joel. I miss him. Maybe this will cheer me up!"

This is what he wrote:

> K, you are the most selfish girl in the entire world. A veritable monster. I offered you friendship and this is how you repay me? I can only imagine how you must treat your enemies. How many straight guys in the whole world do you think there are who like you enough to be your friend without trying to have

sex with you? Maybe zero. Every guy who even sees you on the street wants to have sex with you. You know that. Or if you don't, then you know it unconsciously. You walk through life like a billionaire. That's the sort of confidence you have. Only you're like an arrogant billionaire, spilling hundred-dollar bills from both pockets, squandering her fortune, thinking it will last forever. I am only two years older than you, but I am so much smarter it's ridiculous. As you get older and your looks fade and your ass and tits fall, fewer and fewer guys will want to have sex with you. Until one day you will have no sexual power left. A penniless billionaire! Then your only wealth will be the people whom you have attracted to your life, who know and love the real you. I am one of those people, yet you discard me. At this rate you will die unhappy and alone, and that's probably what you deserve. You have no inner life.

Bye, Joel

I don't know whether I should call him and apologize or just let him go. If I let him go he will tell everybody what a self-centered bitch I am. If I apologize but don't really mean it, he will end up hating me even more. So I should only call him if I am sure that I really want to be his friend.

The funny thing is even though he says he is the only straight guy in the world who doesn't want to bone me, I don't believe him. I think he totally wants to have sex with me. I know that sounds conceited but, come on, can't you sense it from his letter? No guy gets that upset by the behavior of a female friend unless deep down he wants to bone her. I need to think this over. Even though he is an intelligent and honest friend and a great listener, do I really want someone in my life who is so needy?

Friday, February 29, 2008

Today is Leap Year, which only comes around once every seven years. Paul informed me that it is also an old holiday known as Sadie Hawkins Day. This is the day when women are allowed to propose to men. So when Paul was going down on me this afternoon I whispered "Will you marry me?" He laughed so hard he almost choked.

I heart making Paul laugh.

Saturday, March 1, 2008

This evening my mom and Mark were planning their wedding on the dining room table with all of their assembled materials spread out before them. Even though I am dreading the event they looked so happy doing it I decided to join in. I sat down and started looking at the sample invitations and the brochures for ballrooms and the photos of wedding cakes. It was okay for a while. Mark was being the least cynical I have ever seen him and my mom was like a little giggling girl. When Mark got up and went to the kitchen and came back with a cold beer for me, I was blown away. It had been a while. It tastes so much better when you don't have to steal it!

The whole time we were looking over the materials, the big discussion was the date for the wedding. What was the perfect day? We narrowed it down and voted on three choices. June 21 won 3–0. I thought "Hey, that was easy. Maybe we'll become sort of a family now." But then out of nowhere, Mark says something about how the only awkward part of the transition will be where I will sleep in the eight weeks between the wedding and when I leave for college.

I was like "Excuse me?" and that's when they told me that they had decided to sell our house, so that right after the ceremony my mom can move straight into Mark's condo. I was in shock. I have been to his condo. It has three bedrooms, and one of them is a home office and the other is a den with an exercise bike. And even if it had ten bedrooms, so what? I love our house!

I completely freaked out. Where was I going to stay when I come home from college? Where was I going to store all my stuff? What if I want to defer again? Where will I live? I was so disgusted I didn't even speak. I just got up, went to the kitchen, stole two of Mark's beers and escaped to my room. I slammed the door as loudly as possible.

Right now my mom is outside begging me to talk to her. "Sweetheart! Please open up. We need to discuss this! Please!"

I can't decide what cruel thing to scream back. Either "I have a better idea. Go discuss my upcoming suicide with your ugly boyfriend!" or "We don't need anything. You need to haul your big fat ass to bed!"

Oh, well, just lost my chance. She stomped away. She said she can't wait until I start college and get the hell out of her life for a while. Feeling's mutual, bitch!

Sunday, March 2, 2008

Today would have been my father's 55th birthday. If I was a better person I would spend the day with Affie. She called me this week three times but I never called her back. I'm sure it was to invite me over for a memorial dinner. She must be very lonely. But I just can't bear to eat her freaky food and listen to her talk about my dad like he was a combination of George Clooney and Jesus Christ.

I would love to call Paul and tell him about my mom selling our house. I think he will understand my feelings of profound rejection. I will have no real home. No center.

When I come home for Christmas break I will be sleeping on the floor of a home office. I know Paul will give me great advice. I wish I could call him now but of course I can't.

FYI: I also can't call Dan (dumped me) or Rory (hates me again) or Glenn A. Warburg (possible rapist) or Jade (resident evil) or fat Merci (a bore to the core) or Joel (thinks I am resident evil) or Dr. Sherman (thinks I'm seeing a new shrink). No wonder I can't stop crying.

LATER: 8:23 p.m.

I got a nice email from Mglove007 who says the reason why I cannot stop crying is not because my mom is selling the house. It's because today is my father's birthday and I am having a delayed reaction to his tragic death. She is probably right. Thanks for writing, gyrlfriend. You are a peach.

Filyboyz6 sent me an article about a 90-year-old scientist who says global warming is going to get worse and worse much more quickly than anyone thinks. Within 20 years there will be abnormal weather all the time and within 30 Europe will be the Sahara desert. And there's nothing we can do about it! So basically we might as well relax and have fun. Reading this makes me want to have sex with Paul 24/7. Who cares about right and wrong when we're all going to fry? I bet this is not the reaction the scientist wanted!

Friday, March 7, 2008

Sorry I haven't written all week but I have been too happy. It's been absolutely glorious. This is Paul's word. Can you tell? When he paid me tonight he whispered "Wasn't this week glorious?" I whispered back like Katherine Hepburn "Yes, dahling, perfectly glorious!" and he cracked up. I make him laugh all the time. I don't think I have ever been this funny. I've been discovered!

I did not even care that Hillary Clinton won some states on mini Super Tuesday. Paul was really angry about it because it means we're going to have to tolerate her dirty campaign for weeks and weeks to come but I could care less. If I can be naked with Paul every day I don't care if Hitler is president.

Did I really just write that? Hahaha!

Saturday, March 8, 2008

Tons of snow. I am a bored harlot. Even though I am typing right now, deep inside I am sitting on the telephone waiting for it to hatch. Paul said if he could manage to grab a few minutes alone he would call me this weekend. In eight minutes the clock springs ahead one hour. One hour closer to Monday morning when I will be in his arms again.

Sunday, March 9, 2008

All cozy this morning with the world covered in white, I started thinking about what it means to be a good person. Am I a bad person for having sex with a married man or is it just my action that is bad? If I died today and there was really such a thing as Elysium, would I go there or would I end up in Greek hell? I think the answer is pretty obvious. Better pack the ole sunscreen, Katie!

So far there has only been one negative moment with Paul. It's probably nothing but I want to mention it just in case. Wednesday we were lying naked on a beach towel spread over one of the guest room beds and I said "Let's move to a farm and make babies." He laughed and said "But I already have a baby. Wait, come to think of it, I have two!" He started tickling me like I was a little girl. I laughed but I thought it was a pretty disrespectful way to treat me. That's it. The only negative moment. Not bad considering with Rory there was a negative moment every five minutes.

Monday, March 10, 2008

Today I told Paul about my mom selling our house. I'm not sure why it took me so long. Maybe because I don't want to bore him with my juvenile problems. Anyway he was so sympathetic about it that I told him about Mr. Silaggi too. The whole time I talked he just kept shaking his head and saying "You poor thing. You poor thing." I also told him that Dr. Sherman wanted me to write a letter to Mr. Silaggi even if I never send it. Paul said that sounded like an excellent idea, that he was proud of me for doing it and that he would like to read it when I'm finished. Does this mean I actually have to write it now? Shit.

Margaret's job finishes in ten days. She will then go back to being a full-time mom. It will be almost impossible for Paul and me to be alone unless we meet at a motel. Or if he's brave enough to risk it, at my house when my mom's at work. Even though I am an atheist I pray Margaret gets another job soon. If god actually does exist I doubt he will answer an immoral prayer like that. Which means I might have to kill her! LOL!

Tuesday, March 11, 2008

All day my throat hurt and my nose was runny but I pretended I was fine because I knew if Paul knew I had a cold, he would make me go home to protect Cole. Somehow I made it through the day but now I am really ill. Fever and aches. Just took a ton of vitamin C. I must wake up feeling better. I can't miss work!

I was just joking about murdering Margaret. I can't believe how touchy and stupid some of you guys are. Lighten up, yo.

Wednesday, March 12, 2008

Woke up with a 102.7 fever. Head full of boogers. Coughing up chunks of lung. My mom had to call Paul and tell him I wouldn't be coming in today. How weird was that? I think I would die of nervousness if those two ever met. They are only four years apart.

The governor of New York resigned today on TV because he had sex with a whore. I kept watching his wife's face. She reminds me in many ways of Margaret. Very classy and strong. What would Margaret do if she found out about me and Paul? Would she stand by her man, all sad faced and loyal with bowed head, or would she divorce his cheating ass so I could have him all to myself? Only one way to find out. Make sure she catches us. Which won't be easy. Margaret is so type A she never comes home unexpectedly. She always calls first. Paul says she is "the Anti-Surprise." (Get it? Like the Anti-Christ. Ha!) He says this is the main reason their sex life has never been good. She is not spontaneous like I am. I always say yes.

Wouldn't it be amazing if the Spooners got divorced? Even though it would be hard on Cole psychologically, it's not as hard as having your unhappy dad making love to your nanny every time you take a nap, is it? Cole is so young he would barely notice the divorce at this age, I think. He wouldn't be like me who grabbed my dad's leg and had to be dragged across the snowy yard before I let go. I wonder how they would divide up the custody.

I am fantasizing way too much.

My nose just dripped on my keyboard. Yuck.

Thursday, March 13, 2008
During the tiny bits of fever-sleep I had last night, I had the freakiest dreams involving boys I haven't seen or thought of since third grade. The brain is quite a mysterious organ.

Phone ringing. Somebody loves me. Stand by.

It was Margaret saying "Get well soon." Rather than hire a temp nanny during my illness, she decided to only work half days at her job. It's almost finished anyway. I hope spending more time together doesn't make the Spooners fall back in love. She put Paul on for a few seconds, but all he said was "Hurry back, kiddo! We miss you!" He's an excellent actor.

My mom is being super-nice to me, bringing me chicken soup, ice water and vitamins. She even rubbed my feet last night. It's not just because I'm sick. It's also because she feels guilty for selling our house and destroying my feeling of security.

I would never tell her this but it's fun to be babied by her. It brings back memories of the days before I started disappointing her every ten seconds.

Friday, March 14, 2008

I was so much sicker today my mom took me to the doctor. It turns out my flu (which is all over the country now except Florida, and has killed some kids) has turned into bronchitis. I'm on antibiotics now. I hope they work. I'm miserable and lonely.

The stock market is really fucked. I hope Paul doesn't lose too much money. Or he won't he able to afford a good divorce lawyer. Hahaha! Coughcoughcough! Boohoohoo!

Saturday, March 15, 2008

I am finally feeling better and guess what? My hormones are raging. Isn't that wonderful? Aren't I a lucky gyrl? My body, I swear. How can something so beautiful be such a curse?

A humongous crane fell in NYC and crushed a whole apartment building. Can you imagine? You're lying in bed, thinking your life is pretty awesome then a crane comes through your ceiling and smooshes you like a bug? When you think of all the ways your life can end, it's pretty much a miracle we even bother to brush our teeth. Come to think of it, I haven't since yesterday morning!

Sunday, March 16, 2008

I feel so much better today. No aches, no chills, just a slight cough and some cramps. I wonder when I can go back to smoking full-time. Since I've been ill I've only had two or three a day and it's driving me insane. It feels like ants are crawling in the back of my throat. I am going to call Paul right now and tell him I'm coming back to work tomorrow.

Stand by.

. . .

Paul yelled the news to Margaret and she yelled back "Hallelujah!"

Monday, March 17, 2008

Two seconds after Cole fell asleep, Paul and I started kissing. We didn't even make it to the guest room. We made love on the hallway floor. It was incredibly hot. When it was over I told him my period is coming any minute so we'd better do it as much as we can while we still have the chance.

"Not a problem," he said.

I didn't even know how much I missed Paul until I was in his arms again. His mouth, his smell, his touch. I think he's falling in love with me too. He never stops smiling.

Tonight my mom celebrated St. Patrick's Day by serving her world-famous corned beef and cabbage (which I hate) and a six-pack of yummy Irish ale. We drank two ales each and pretty soon Mark started talking in an Irish accent. I couldn't stop laughing. He thought it was because he was so darned funny but actually I was laughing at him. And the harder I laughed the more Irish he acted. Imagine a frog-faced man with no neck, a big belly and a green ski sweater bouncing around in his chair twirling his mustache and doing the worst Irish accent, while thinking he's adorable. That's why I almost had a heart attack. I cannot believe my mother would destroy our cozy life for a man this insipid.

My mother has decided that the answer to the difficult question "What to do with Katie?" is that from the time the house is sold until I go to college (she hopes), I will sleep on a fancy inflatable mattress in Mark's den. She has heard they're really comfortable.

I replied "Or you could just find me a refrigerator box."

That's honestly how I feel. Homeless. She is such a typical middle-aged woman. They talk all feminist and independent but as soon as a man walks into their lives, they drop everything. Even their kids.

Tuesday, March 18, 2008

Paul and I watched Barack Obama's speech about racism. It was amazing. Near the end I thought Paul had caught my cough, but I looked over and he was crying. I don't think I have ever seen a grown man cry before except on TV and movies. Paul has a beautiful soul.

Later I asked Paul why he cried and he said because it was the greatest speech ever delivered by an American politician, even greater than the great speeches of Martin Luther

King, because it was in prose not poetry, and it is much harder to move people with prose. He said that in a perfect world Obama would be president until the end of time. Wow. Considering he works with money all day and used to be a Republican, that's a pretty big deal for him to say about a Democrat. Wait, wait, this is a bitter truth, but I forget which number: *Every human being is a paradox.*

Speaking of which, one weird moment today reminded me of when Paul called me his baby and tickled me. We were making love and he reached down, hooked me by the knee and turned me over. Right as my face touched the towel he said "Usually I don't believe in tummy time. But in this case I'll make an exception." I know it was just a joke but isn't it disrespectful to talk about your lover like she's your baby? Or am I being oversensitive because of hormones?

Dan and I were watching a film once called *Women in Love* based on the controversial feminist novel by D.H. Lawrence, and he said "Women love romance. Men love pornography." What if this is true of me and Paul? What if I am having a romance and he's having a porno? Wouldn't that be tragic? I would be so humiliated.

Thursday, March 20, 2008

I haven't told anyone. I will tell you. My period still hasn't come yet. What's scaring the shit out of me is that I just called Merci Gregoris who had an abortion senior year and I asked what it felt like to be pregnant and she said "It feels like a period that never comes." That's exactly how I feel. I feel weird and crampy and my boobs are sore but it can't be normal PMS because I am not crying for no reason. AAARRRGGHH!

First day of spring.

Margaret's job finishes tomorrow.

Saturday, March 22, 2008

I was so nervous taking my home pregnancy test just now that I messed up and peed all over the toilet seat and my hand. The second test I was more careful with and it showed a very, very, very faint blue line. I almost couldn't see it. I hope it was a mistake. On the directions it says nothing about very, very, very faint blue lines. It just says that the second blue line should look exactly like the first one. Well it didn't. It was fainter. I'm too tired and scared to go out and buy another test.

. . .

Every time I turn on the TV people are talking smack about Obama. Why do they keep calling him black? He isn't black. He is biracial. (Do you know why you shouldn't use the word "mulatto"? Because it means "mule." Half horse, half donkey. Paul teaches me stuff like this all the time.) I honestly think the white racists don't want to think about the fact that his mother is white. They don't get how important this fact is. They don't get him at all. They don't understand that he is the human version of our diverse society.

Sunday, March 23, 2008

Took two more tests just now and both showed very faint blue lines. Fuuuuuck! I never thought I would be one of those typical stupid teenage girls who gets pregnant. Actually I'm not all that typical because I don't even know who the father is. It could be Rory, Dan or Paul. I am extra stupid!

What's really embarrassing is that last Monday I told Paul my period was coming any minute, so every day this week he asked me if it had started yet. I didn't want him to worry that I was pregnant, so on Thursday when he walked me to the door, I whispered that it had just started. (I was sure it was going to any minute.) This means that when I get to work tomorrow he's going to think it's pretty much over and he's going to want to make love. I could do it but if I am going to get an abortion wouldn't it be a smart idea not to go to the clinic filled with man juice? What do I do? Make him wear a condom the day after my period supposedly ended? It will make him think I have an STD. (I don't.) What I am trying to say is "Happy Easter, Katie!"

My mom is cooking lamb for dinner, my all-time favorite. I don't use the mint sauce. I put fresh lime on it. Yum. I must remember not to watch a video of lambs being slaughtered and fake-humped right before I sit down to eat.

When I woke up this morning there was a dark-chocolate bunny rabbit in bright yellow foil at the foot of my bed. I was so happy and grateful that I called my mother "Mommy" all day. She asked what had gotten into me and I said "Nothing, I just temporarily like you. Enjoy it!"

Monday, March 24, 2008
Today was Margaret's first day back and she already had a job interview scheduled for 2:00. (It's for a major job that would take months.) It would normally have made Paul really angry that she was ready to leave Cole again so soon, but now that we are in love, I don't think he cares at all. Besides Cole is used to being with just us during the day.

As soon as Margaret left, we started kissing.

I stopped him and said "We can't. Don't be mad."

He said "Why not? Your period's over, isn't it?"

"I have a urinary track infection. Nothing major. I took the medicine today. It'll be gone soon."

He smiled. "It's all my fault. I can't keep my hands off you."

"Back at ya, buddy! Back at ya!"

He laughed at my old-fashioned expression (which I got from my dad) then he took my hand and started rubbing his bulge with it. I knew what he wanted. I pushed him back on the bed. When he came, it felt so good he covered his face with a pillow and screamed into it. I'm dead serious. I am a master!

Wednesday, March 26, 2008

I can tell Margaret is getting depressed already and wishes she had a new job. She doesn't admit it, of course. She pretends that she missed Cole every minute and that it's a blast getting to spend more time with him.

I was so lonely tonight that I almost called Nick, my disgusting one night stand. Instead I called Joel Seidler. Yes, his letter was full of rage but I hurt his feelings and I deserved it. I was sure that if I was really sweet to him and sincerely apologized for being so selfish, he would forgive me. Well, I didn't get the chance to find out because his mom answered.

Her voice was shaky. She was about to start bawling. She said Joel was in the hospital. I asked what happened.

"Aw, who knows? These shrinks are a bunch of witch doctors if you ask me." She sounded New Yorky and kind of crazy. "I'm not telling you anything you don't know, right? I mean, you're good friends. You know about his depression, right?"

"Oh, yeah, totally. We talk about it all the time. But he was getting so much better."

"Well, he relapsed. Made another attempt. Pills this time. The pills his doctors gave him. I thought only girls took pills. I was the one who found him. Scariest moment of my life. I thought he was dead."

"Can I visit him?"

"Maybe in a couple of weeks. Right now they don't even want me and Sid there. They got to get his chemistry straightened out."

The way she talked about Joel, I swear you would have thought he was her boyfriend instead of her son. She is way too into him. Maybe that's why he took the pills.

Joel's mother gave me the name of the hospital. As soon as I figure out what to say I will send Joel a card. Normally I would just email him but they don't allow electronics.

I took another test. The faint blue line isn't faint anymore. ☹

Thursday, March 27, 2008

Rory dropped by tonight without calling. He brought weed, thinking that would be enough to make me at least be nice to him, if not bone him. Normally he would be right (ha!) but no way am I going to get high while I'm pregnant. When I said no thanks, he got really suspicious. I tried to lie my way out of it but he knows me too well. So I had to confess. He took my pregnancy news in the worst possible way. His skin turned bright red and he broke into the biggest smile. He assumed that he was the father and that I was going to keep it. Can you believe how clueless he is?

I deaded that shit superfast.

"Whoa, whoa," I said "slow down. The baby isn't yours and even if it was, I'm not keeping it."

He stared at me in shock then walked over and looked out the dark window. He didn't say a word for a long time. His jaw moved like he was chewing something small. It was the maddest I've ever seen him. It was scary. He really hates abortion. (It's because his mom wanted to abort him. Did I already tell you that?) Finally he started walking around the room in circles like an animal at the zoo making uglier and uglier faces. I got the feeling that if it wasn't for the pregnancy he would have beaten the shit out of me right there.

Finally he talked.

"If you knew you were getting an abortion, why did you even bother telling me about it?"

"Because you were pressuring me to get stoned, and there's no way I was going to do that."

"Why not? Who cares if it hurts the baby if you're killing it anyway?"

Good point. The answer was impossible for me to admit. It's that deep down I'm hoping that either Dan or Paul will want me to keep it. If this happens I will not abort. Of course the worst thing would be if one of these men said okay and then the baby was born with red hair and freckles. I would be so busted. Obviously I couldn't tell Rory this. So I asked him to leave. He said no way, not until I told him who the father was. I told him it was none of his business. He made a furious face and stuck out his hands like claws at me. When I screamed and covered my face, he stormed out and slammed the door.

Friday, March 28, 2008

I had a dream last night that there were two babies growing inside me. The doctor gave me color photographs of them in the womb. One was milky pink and smiling and looked really healthy. The other one was one stained yellowish brown from cigarettes. I started crying because I had destroyed one of my babies. Then I woke up.

I know I should abort this weekend without even telling Dan or Paul. That would be the most mature thing to do. I wish I had someone to go with me. It's a tragic thing to do alone.

Stand by.

I just googled "I had an abortion." I couldn't believe what came up. Many, many stories from girls who had abortions and now regretted it All they do now is lie in bed crying, contemplating suicide. But then I noticed that all of these tales were posted on prolife websites. No wonder! They're never going to print stories from girls who are happy they aborted. Now I will google "abortion" and "best thing."

Stand by.

Not as many matches came up, because obviously someone who has an abortion and then goes on to have an awesome life isn't going to waste time posting about it. But there were many brave inspiring tales. It was marvelous to hear from women who said that abortion saved their lives. I can't wait for mine now!

That was a joke. I am scared shitless. More than anything in the world I want to tell Paul I'm pregnant but I keep chickening out.

Saturday, March 29, 2008

I emailed Dan this morning and said that I really needed to talk to him as soon as possible. Five minutes later the email bounced back. He's blocked my address! Part of me was impressed that he could be this strong but the other half was really offended and furious, so I got into my car and drove over to his house.

On the way I saw Jade for the first time since she betrayed me. She was standing outside a Starbucks, hanging all over this greasy ugly guy covered in tats. They looked like they had both been up all night having a three-way with a crack pipe. It's scary because she used to be so vain and now she looks like a zombie. (She has zits and her hair is in a total Winehouse.) She stared right at me but I'm not even sure she knew who I was. Of course I felt bad for her, but it's hard not to think she deserves it. The ugliness on her insides has taken over the outside.

No one was home at Dan's. Looking back on it, thank god! I left a note in the mailbox telling him to call me asap. I signed it "Your favorite student."

Sunday, March 30, 2008

Driving around with the windows down and the roof open to prevent myself from throwing up, I drove past the hospital where Joel is locked up. It could so easily be me in there. I still haven't sent him a card. He must hate me.

Why do they call it morning sickness? It's morning, noon and night sickness! Maybe they're afraid if they told us we'd never have babies.

I guess Jade saw me drive by yesterday. She just left me a voice mail. She said she wants to talk things out. Some things can't be talked out. And sometimes it's not even worth telling the person who hurt you that this is one of those things that can't be talked out.

Dan has not called.

Monday, March 31, 2008

Paul turned 45 today. I didn't know what to give him. How about a brand-new bouncing baby? Instead I gave him a silly card that he opened in front of Margaret. Inside I wrote "Thanks for being such an awesome boss. xo Katie." Margaret read it over his shoulder and said in a totally casual way "Oh, that's sweet." Boy, she really doesn't suspect. How could she be so oblivious? (I hope that's the word.)

The second she went upstairs I gave Paul his present. In the kitchen. It made him soooooo happy. After it was over I asked him how it felt to be 45. He said it feels exactly like being 18 only when you get out of a chair your back is stiff.

Then I gave him the second part of his present. A poem I wrote. He said it was really beautiful and very impressive. Then he said "Now I suppose I have to burn it." My feelings were hurt of course. Just like after I gave Dan a pic of me and he handed it back. But I knew he was absolutely right. Since I have it on my computer I didn't need the copy I gave him, so we ripped it up and pushed it all the way to the bottom of the garbage.

I looked up just now and my mom was staring at me from my door. I asked her what she wanted. She said she's worried about me. That I am way too thin lately and I've been dressing like a streetwalker. I told her that I am thin because I haven't felt like eating since Dan and I broke up. And how I dress is none of her business.

She said "But, darling, you left the house tonight in a coat, a halter top, torn tights and sneakers. You weren't even wearing a skirt or pants."

"And every guy who saw me at the liquor store popped a boner." I laughed like a cocky bitch.

She made a sad clown face.

I said "Go! Go! Go!"

Tuesday, April 1, 2008

You will never guess! I told Dan I'm pregnant! He wants to keep the baby! He's going to dump Martine! I asked him to marry me the same weekend my mom marries Mark and he said yes! A double wedding will get us discounts! Once the baby is old enough for day care, I can attend Dan's college for free as the wife of a professor! And even though there's no such thing, we will live happily ever after!

April Fools.

Gotcha!

tee hee

Wednesday, April 2, 2008

Only one person asked me to post the poem I wrote for Paul. I was kind of disappointed that more of you weren't interested. Anyway, ppmarin, here it is. If you don't like it, please lie and say you did.

FOR PAUL ON HIS 45TH BIRTHDAY

Napping on the sofa

near baby boy napping

in his bouncy chair.

Two separate lives
lying so close for a while
until you both wake up
and become
father and son again.
May you always be like this,
sleeping close and waking close,
sharing nearly all of your lives.
I wish I could
share them too!

Today I was doing god knows what on my computer when I randomly google searched "stupid depressing shit." I only got 14 matches. I would have thought many more. I clicked on one at random. This is what came up from some chick's blog called "Daily Random Things Happening."

human beings are stupid depressing shit i know i shouldn't care about strangers so much but i do and everytime i meet another fake phony depressing stupid shit human being it makes death seem all the more tasty exit stage left o-feelia! i am way too emotional to live on this dirty green ball but not strong enough to leave its predicament! horns of a dilemma! horny devil horns! one of the great things about ranting here is that no one reads it! 'cept friends who began blocking me out years ago fingers in ears peas and carrots peace and carrots yet somehow i always come out the other end and see the silver lining altho even that is getting old real old better start planning my own funferall!

I wish I were as brave and raw and insane as this chick. I hide my deepest and ugliest emotions. I think I'm afraid if I share them with you, you will stop reading and I will just be a pathetic undiscovered gyrl typing alone in her room.

Okay, I will answer a quiz for real this time. No joking. No lies. This is the real me.

ABSOLUTELY NO LYING OR JOKING QUIZ

Q. When was last time you cried?
A. One minute ago.

Q. What and when was your last meal?
A. Fried rice forty minutes ago. I forced it down to keep from throwing up.

Q. Have you ever dated the same person twice?
A. I have never dated.

Q. Have you ever kissed someone and regretted it?
A. Nick Dempster and many others. The worst was Tim

Lovelace. 16 when I was 10. My first tongue kiss. What a perv.

Q. Have you ever been in love?

A. Twice.

Q. Have you ever lost someone?

A. Dad, Rory, Dan, and, soon, baby. Then probably Paul.

Please list five things you did in the past three hours:

1. Swallowed snot and tears.
2. Looked at my stomach sideways in the mirror.
3. Dialed the clinic and hung up.
4. Googled "up for adoption."
5. Watched a disgusting Japanese porn video online. I could describe it, but that would not be fair to the girl or to the octopus.

Please list three people you completely trust:

1. Paul
2. My mom
3.

Please list three things you want to do before you die:

1. be discovered
2. be truly loved
3. have three kids

Q. Do you believe in love at first sight?

A. Not for me.

Q. Is there something you want to tell someone?

A. Yes but he is probably dead by now.

Q. What is your favorite thing in your room?

A. My heart.

Q. What is your least favorite thing in your room?

A. My heart.

Q. Have you ever been drunk and thrown up?

A. Duh.

Thursday, April 3, 2008

Being pregnant is like being seasick and you can't get off the boat. The smell of bubble gum, deodorant, scented candles, Cole's pee and poo, even Paul's sperm, all make me want to vomit till my toes come out my mouth.

Friday, April 4, 2008

I am goig to cal Dan right now th8s minute. I am drunk don't give a shit what answers.

. . .

Stand byy

What happened
    May I please speak to DanN?
    Who may I zay oo izzz calling?
    His favorite student.
    Daniel for you! A zzztudent!
    Shoesteps.
    Dan sauys Hello?
    Hi it's me asshole. I'm pregnant. And since the baby is
yours I thought maybe befor I get an abortion you'd like to
discuss it.
    Amber please. You know better. Call during my office
hours. 4 til 6 Moday thru Friday. Good night!
    Click.
    Just lovely the way he rolls Right?
    I HATE HIM!

Saturday, April 5, 2008
Isn't Dan curious what I am going to do with his baby? He is
a major coward not to call me back. Unless he thinks I'm an
alcoholic liar.

I watched a show on Martin Luther King. They showed a
film of him giving a speech the night before he died. It was
like he knew he was going to get shot! What a beautiful

voice. Obama is his son. Keep hope alive please. If not for me, at least for the world.

Sunday, April 6, 2008

Dan is pathetic and weak. I never saw it before. I was blinded by love. I feel like going over there and ruining his life. Instead I write poetry.

> Now all I do is eat
> And fill up on defeat.
> I plead guilty to all charges
> While my shame just enlarges.

Monday, April 7, 2008

Paul asked me three times today what's wrong and I kept saying "Nothing, I'm just really run-down." He didn't believe me. He knows I am depressed and he assumes it's because of him, because we are hardly ever alone anymore. He feels guilty about it and then all he wants to do is make love every chance we get so I will be happy again. For example, Margaret went out to meet another possible client. (I hope she gets the job!) The second she was gone Paul dragged me upstairs. Boy, was he overdue! Ha! I was not into it at all because of my condition but I pretended that I was.

. . .

I can't stand this. I'm getting it aborted this Saturday morning no matter what.

Tuesday April 8, 2008

I'm sad today . . . so so sad today . . . so so-so today . . . so sad daddy . . . sad is so today . . . sad sad daddy for reals . . . .

Wednesday, April 9, 2008

I made another abortion appointment for this Saturday at 10:00. I am so relieved. Just to make sure I really go this time, I drank two beers after dinner and am no longer worrying about how much I smoke.

Phone ringing. Somebody loves me. Stand by.

Affie. Inviting me over for dinner Friday night. I haven't seen her once since my dad's funeral. She sounded lonely. Seeing her will keep me from sitting home in my room and getting shit-faced on the eve of my abotion. Ha! Funny typo. Is that what sistas get? Abotions? Ha! Wait, they don't. They have the kids. And then work three jobs to support them. They are brave. That's what I would do if I weren't a spoiled white girl.

. . .

I hate my guts right now. I am breaking up with myself. I am sorry Katie but I need space.

Friday, April 11, 2008

I was scared that it would be painful for me to be back in my dad's apartment again. I thought when I saw his stuff I might really lose it. Well, I didn't. Because none of his stuff was there! The place looked exactly the way it did the first time I ever had dinner there, way back when my dad and Affie first met. My dad's TV chair was gone. None of his sports books were lined up on the window sill. Even the smell of his cigarettes had vanished!

I was so shocked I didn't say anything. When Affie went to the kitchen to get me some Indian tea, I walked into the bedroom. His whole half of the closet was filled with Affie's foreign robes. She had wiped my dad away like he never existed! I felt like puking. Not just because I was disgusted with what she did. Also because everything stank of flowery incense.

When Affie came in, I asked her what happened to my dad's stuff.

"Goodwill."

"You mean, you gave it away?"

"What else could I do? I certainly couldn't sell it. It wasn't worth very much."

She was smiling in this dopey way. Like brown Mona Lisa with a mustache.

"I just thought maybe you might want to keep some of his stuff around to remember him by."

"Oh, I'll remember him, little girl."

What did that mean? Was she being sarcastic?

I replied "Plus maybe I wanted some of his things. Did that ever occur to you?"

"Of course. I set a few things aside."

She reached into a carved Indian box made of many different woods and pulled out a bundle of red velvet. I thought maybe she was going to give me something really special. I didn't know what exactly but I had that fantasy. She opened the cloth and carefully handed me my dad's wristwatch, his driver's license, his car keys on a Greenbay Packers key ring, and his wedding ring. The objects were so grimy and cheap—so him—it made his life and death seem even sadder. I started to bawl. Affie hugged me. I got snot on her dress and she didn't care.

I hung out with her for another couple of hours, eating her surrealistic food and trying to think of things to talk about. It was difficult because we don't have anything in common and I was still really nauseous. Right when I said I needed to go home and get some sleep, she said something weird that I didn't understand.

She said "What a shame he didn't leave that silly card where it was."

"What card?"

"The one you gave him with his Christmas gift." She pointed to the empty space where his chair used to be. "If he had listened to me, he'd be alive right now, sitting right there."

"What the hell are you talking about?"

She said the day my dad had his accident she was cleaning up and found the Christmas present I gave him at the bottom of his closet. She put the underwear and socks away and threw out the box. Later that night my dad freaked out because inside the box was the card I gave him. She didn't understand what the big deal was. If the card had meant so much to him, why hadn't he saved it? They had a big fight about it. Affie admitted to me that she was a little jealous he cared so much about the card because he never cared about hers.

She went to bed angry. In the middle of the night she heard him moving around in the dark, putting on shoes. She asked where he was going at midnight and he said "To pick through the garbage, like your cousins back in Calcutta." When she woke up an hour later, the room was windy and freezing. She got out of bed and walked to the kitchen. The back door was wide open. That's when she saw him lying at the bottom of the wooden steps.

I started crying again. I think Affie assumed I was crying because I believed my card had led to his death and I felt in some way responsible. I was actually crying because I thought my dad never read my cards. But I kept writing them anyway because it's the polite thing to do. Now I knew he read them in private. Does this mean he loved me in private too? Why else would he go outside in the freezing cold? Did he secretly save all the cards I gave him? If so where are they now? Did Affie give them to Goodwill? But if he loved me how come he never asked me a single question about my life? How come he never hugged me or said nice things? How come we never did anything together? The saddest thing was that I knew I would never know the answers to any of these questions.

After I stopped crying I told Affie some of my theories about why my dad was so mean to me. She semi-agreed with one of them. She thinks after I became a young woman it made him uncomfortable. But not because I look like my mom. She doesn't think I do. She thinks he was just uncomfortable because I am so beautiful. WTF? I had no idea what this meant. Did she mean he was uncomfortable because he was attracted to me?! It was such a disgusting thought I didn't even ask her to explain. I just said I was dead tired and had a doctor's appointment in the morning, which was true. I cried all the way home. I wanted so badly to call Paul for comfort, but I knew it was impossible.

Saturday, April 12, 2008

This morning I woke up thinking that in about two hours I would be getting an abortion, but my mom showed up at my door and said she had made me a 10:00 appointment to see Dr. Elaine Sherman. Turns out my mom's known for a long time that I stopped therapy. She was going to just let it slide but I've been acting so offensively lately that she changed her mind When I started to say no, she said either I go to therapy or I can pack my bags and move the hell out.

LATER: 3:12 p.m.

The second I got into Dr. Sherman's office I started bawling. I told her that lately I've been crying way too much and that I have been thinking about killing myself and that I need some meds to make me stop.

She said "You're not clinically depressed. Depressed people don't cry the way you are. Depressed people sit in the dark unable to move a muscle. You don't need drugs. You're grieving. For your dead father. For your lost innocence. You need to keep crying until you run out of tears."

Whoa, right?

I kept on sobbing without even saying anything and that was fine with her. She handed me a box of Kleenex and just sat there watching. (Pretty easy way to make money.) Later she asked me if I ever got an answer to my letter to Mr. Silaggi. I told her I never wrote it. She handed me a pen and paper and told me to start writing. I told her I couldn't. She said "Of course you can." Well she was right. I did it easily. She liked it very much. She told me that whether I mail it or not is irrelevant. All that matters is that I have now put my feelings into words.

If you care, here it is:

Dear Mr. Silaggi:

You probably thought I forgot. Or maybe you just hoped I did. Well I didn't. I remember everything you did to me. Some-times I wondered if maybe you forgot. Then I realized that was impossible. I was just a confused little girl but you were a grown man at the time you molested me. I feel sorry for your wife and children. You are lucky that my dad is dead and that my mom is the non-violent type or you would be in serious trouble right now. I want you to think about what you did to me and the cruel sickness of it. You killed my childhood. I am suicidal today and a lot of it has to do with you. If you are a Christian and I think you are, then you know what awaits you.

Yours truly,

Little Katie

(Kampenfelt)

. . .

I was too scared to tell Dr. Sherman about my pregnancy. And why bother if it's going to be terminated anyway? I told her I would see her in two weeks. She said why not next Saturday and I said because I have a previous engagement.

LATER: 1:46 a.m.

I can't believe what I just did. I walked to the corner and mailed the letter to Mr. Silaggi at his lake house. I wonder if he goes there anymore. He is probably dead and the letter will bounce back.

Since some of you asked, all I wrote in my dad's card was "From your favorite and only daughter, xoxox K." Nothing worth cracking your skull over.

Sunday, April 13, 2008

Driving around in the warm rain today I did something you will think is stupid but was probably the smartest thing I have ever done. I went to Elysium Books. For those of you who discovered my blog recently and are too lazy to go back and read it from the beginning, I used to work there but I had to quit when my mom's fiancé found out that my boss, Glenn A. Warburg, was a registered sexual offender. My mom ordered me to quit my job and I obediently did.

Anyway, driving around today I thought about Glenn and how wonderful I felt whenever we talked. He made me feel intelligent, serious and full of potential. He was such a positive influence on me and that's exactly what I need right now. I need transcendence! The next thing I knew I was turning the steering wheel and heading toward his store. I parked two blocks away so that I would have time to think it over and back out.

As I got closer and closer I got more and more scared but then I saw the warm light shining from inside his shop and I instantly stopped worrying. I felt safe. I just knew that no matter what terrible crime Glenn committed in the past, he had changed. I trusted my heart. I cupped my hands on the foggy window. Way in back, the door was open and I could see Glenn typing away on his computer. I felt so excited, like when you dump a boyfriend but then decide to get back together with him. Instead of just calling to tell him the good news, you show up at his bedroom window in the middle of the night and completely blow his mind. That's how I felt before I rang the bell. When Glenn saw me standing there, he was so happy. He gave me the hugest smile ever.

"Why, if it isn't my favorite person in the whole wide world!" he said.

He hurried me inside and hugged me like I was his long-lost daughter. Considering I only worked for him for like a week, this was very sweet. We sat down in the back office and he gave me a cup of hot mint tea and a handful of vanilla cookies. He told me to tell him all about my life. I told him everything except the sexual stuff (that doesn't leave much! ha!) and for a while that was okay but then he started smiling at me in a really suspicious way.

"Katie, something's wrong. Come on, what is it? Spill the beans."

"How come you know everything?"

"Because I'm older than you are. When you're older, you'll know everything too. Especially about young people. It's easy to read kids."

I liked being called a kid. Everyone is always telling me how mature I am and I'm sick of it. Plus it's not true. Inside I am six.

"Before I tell you," I said, "there's something we need to talk about first if we're going to be true friends."

"Okay."

"I didn't quit for the reason I gave you. I quit because my mom's fiancé found you on a registered sexual offenders website."

Total silence.

I looked at him, scared of what I would see. His whole face had changed. But not in a freaky serial killer way. In a nice way. Everything was softer and more innocent. Like he was relieved not to have a secret anymore. Which made sense. What's worse than keeping a shameful secret?

"I wondered about that," he said.

"I wanted to talk to you about it, but my mom would have grounded me until the end of time."

"She was worried about you."

"Hello? I'm a girl."

"I noticed. Then why are you here? What changed?"

"I missed you. And things have been terrible lately. I thought maybe you could give me some advice."

"I'd be happy to. If I can."

"But first you have to tell me what you did. What your sex crime was."

Glenn just stared then pointed to the Kent Lights sticking out of my purse and asked if he could bum one.

"You smoke?"

"I'm what's known at Nicotine Anonymous as a periodic."

"You start and stop?"

"That's right." He lit one up and inhaled deeply, smiling like he was breathing in an entire bakery. "Well, I guess the first thing I should tell you is that when I was your age I was a mess. I drank vodka for breakfast and never met a drug I didn't like. I robbed houses and sold pot for a living. I was busted for both. To avoid jail time I joined the Marines."

He laughed at the face I made. It was really hard to picture him with a buzz cut and a machine gun.

"After I was dishonorably discharged I moved to California. The desert. The military had changed me. I was still a mess, but now I was a violent one. One night I got hammered and went to the house of a young prostitute I knew. She was expensive and I couldn't afford her. She knew it. She tried to push me out the door. I demanded a drink. I remember her handing me a bottle. Then I blacked out. Later, when I woke up in jail, I had no choice but to take the girl's word for what happened. And the word of the emergency room doctor. I didn't rape her in the way most people would define the word. But I beat her up pretty badly, and there was a sexual act involved that I'd rather not go into."

"How long were you in jail?"

"Thirteen and a half years. I educated myself. I was released seven years ago this August. Haven't touched a drink or a drug in almost fifteen."

"I knew you'd changed."

"I have. But it's still one day at a time. If I picked up a drink, who knows what I'd turn into? Actually I do. I do know."

He gave me a sad smile. We just sat there and listened to the rain for a while. Then he reached over. I thought he was going to hold my hand. Which scared the shit out of me. But he just took another cigarette.

"Now tell me what's wrong. You look terrible. You're wasting away."

I lit a cigarette and told him everything that's happened since I quit working for him. As usual he was an awesome listener. Every now and then he'd ask a question. He didn't seem to care very much about my break-up with Rory, although he did make a worried face when I told him how Rory gets violently jealous sometimes. When I started telling him about Dan, he stopped me and suggested that we continue this at a restaurant a few blocks away. We walked together under a dorky red umbrella. We ate pasta and salads while I continued my story. He didn't have that big a reaction to Dan but when I got to Paul he started chewing slower. When I got to the part where Paul and I made love for the first time, his eyes sort of bulged.

"What? You think he's a dirtbag? That's what Dan called him."

He said he didn't want to comment yet. He told me to finish. When I got to the pregnancy, he stopped chewing.

"And you're smoking?" he said.

I told him since I was going to have an abortion it didn't really matter.

"Oh, I see. I thought you were going to ask for my advice but you've made up your mind."

"Pretty much. I'm too young and crazy to have a baby. But I keep canceling my appointments. I'm scared to go alone."

"You want me to go with you?"

"Would you?"

"Sure. On certain conditions."

I felt this weird vibration run up my arm and I got a flash that he was going to ask me to blow him or something. I know that's totally insane but it's how my mind works. Is it because of what Mr. Silaggi did to me? I will definitely discuss this with Dr. Sherman.

Glenn's conditions for helping me:
1) I must promise never to speak to Dan again.
2) I must quit my job and never speak to Paul again.
3) I must go on the birth control pill.
4) I must attend three AA meetings in the next three weeks.

Numbers 1, 3, and 4 are easy. Number 2 is the biggie, of course. I was afraid to admit this to Glenn so I said "But if I quit my job, what will I do for money? Paul says we're headed for a big recession."

"You can come work for me again."

"My mom would kill me."

"You're eighteen now. You don't need her permission."

"She'll kick me out of the house."

"That's fine. I have a room above my garage. It's not much. Pretty crummy, actually. The previous owner used it as a ceramics studio. But I bet you could make it pretty. Take it. I won't even charge you rent. You can mow the lawn or something. Feed my cats."

I couldn't believe it. It's so much better than sleeping on a blow-up mattress in Mark Aubichon's den. This way I can save up money and if I decide not to start college in the fall,

I'll have a place to live. My mom will be pissed but so what? There's nothing she can do about it. But am I strong enough to break up with Paul? I really do love him.

Monday, April 14, 2008

On the TV they are ragging on Barack. He said people in the Midwest are bitter at being unemployed and poor and that's why they love their guns and god. Before, I was afraid someone was going to assassinate him but now I think why should they bother when they can just destroy him with words? If he doesn't win the nomination, there's no way I'm voting. Ever.

Tuesday, April 15, 2008

Glenn scheduled my abortion for tomorrow morning at a clinic out of town so there won't be any gossip. I called Margaret to quit, but I chickened out. Instead I told her that I had sprained my ankle really badly and that I couldn't come into work tomorrow. Since she is still unemployed she didn't mind at all.

Many girls think having a baby will make all their dreams come true. They think a baby will give them unconditional love 24/7. As a nanny I understand that this is just a fantasy.

In reality it's the exact opposite. You give and give and give to a baby all day every day. They don't start loving you back for a long time.

Wednesday, April 16, 2008

Glenn closed up his shop and we drove to my abortion in his big old yellow Caddy with a red leather interior. I was so nervous we hardly talked. We just listened to oldies. Real oldies. Sinatra and Nat King Cole. The songs went perfect with his car.

The clinic was glassy and modern and looked more like an office building than a hospital. There were metal detectors at the door. While one guard wanded me, another one dug inside my purse for a bomb. Inside everything was white. If I ran an abortion clinic I would make it the exact opposite. Cozy and comfortable. A lot of wood and nice rugs.

The people in the waiting room were a lot browner than the people you normally see around here. Not just black and Mexican but also people that looked like they were from completely different countries. The white people were everything from a freaky chick with tats all upside her neck and hair like a parrot to a really rich-looking blonde lady in Prada. I was shocked that so many people of such diversity get abortions on a weekday.

They gave me a clipboard and a ton of forms to fill out. I did not fill in the credit card info because I was paying in cash. People were definitely staring at us. Either because they thought Glenn was the father of the baby and they judged him for it or because they thought he was my dad and that it was kind of weird/cool he was taking me.

About an hour later the nurse called out my name. They took me in and drew some blood. Then I went back out and sat with Glenn some more. He was reading an article about colic which is a disease that makes babies cry nonstop. He said that sometimes, because of colic, nannies and parents lose their shit and shake their babies to death. Cole never had it, thank god.

A little while later a cold-faced blonde nurse with huge tits came in and took me away. I stripped and put on a robe. There was a big photo of the Grand Canyon on the wall. (Or was it a woman's vagina after having a baby? Hahahaha!) I sat down on a table covered in paper. She stayed and watched while this older lady with glasses came in to do the ultrasound.

"Anything you want to know about your fetus?" the lady asked while she was lowering me down on the table.

I could not believe she asked me this. I looked at the first nurse like "Is this bitch for real?" and she made a sorry face and whispered "Some patients want to know if it's twins."

"Well, not me."

The older lady stuck this greasy long instrument up

me. Unfortunately it did not vibrate. Ha! When she was finished she gave me a pain pill and took me into a small operating room. This older lady turned out to be the coolest person ever. She told me she had two abortions when she was still in high school and that the place where she had them treated her like shit so when she became a nurse she wanted to work in a woman's clinic that treated girls better than the way she was treated. It felt so good to have someone to talk to who understood how scary it all was. We both agreed we would kill for a smoke right about now.

When the doctor finally came in, she was younger and prettier than I pictured. Maybe 35, brown hair, fancy glasses, slightly buck teeth. She was kind and friendly but I was too nervous to chat. I just wanted it over with. She asked if I wanted to be put to sleep or get a local. I picked the local because I didn't want Glenn to have to wait too long.

The whole thing took, I swear, about nine minutes. At least that's how it seemed. And it hurt a little for maybe half a minute. I've heard girls say it's like pulling a tooth. Trust me, it's not. A pulled tooth hurts way worse. The worst part was the creepy noise the machine made.

Afterwards I wanted to leave immediately but the rules state that the patient has to lie down for 30 minutes. I guess in case of bleeding. There were magazines but I just laid there and stared at the ceiling. I couldn't believe how not sad I felt. I was going to have a new life now. When time was up they gave me this big sort of maxi-pad and some birth control pills. They said I could not have sex for two to four weeks. I had no idea! If I break my word and see Paul again, how am I going to explain it?

When I got out of the clinic I turned my phone back on and there was a text from Paul. He said he hoped my ankle wasn't too bad and that he missed me.

"Something important?" Glenn asked.

"No, just my mom. She's all excited. She found the perfect place to have her wedding."

Driving back, Glenn and I stopped for waffles and he told me stories about the Japanese in World War Two and how cruel they were to our captured troops. They marched and marched them for hundreds of miles and if a troop got sleepy, they killed them on the spot, either shooting or beheading them. At the end of the war when they knew the American army was approaching, the Japanese needed to cover up their war crimes. So they put all the prisoners into air raid shelters then poured in gasoline and burned them alive. He said if we learned anything from it, it should have been not to lower ourselves to their barbaric standards.

LATER: 1:06 a.m.

Tonight I recuperated in bed watching the Democratic debate but it was not relaxing at all. The whole time I wanted to crawl into the TV set and choke Hillary to death. Anything to stop her from being so mean. I love Barack with all my heart. I doubt I would ever commit suicide if he was president, no matter how depressed I was, because I would always be able to picture a better life.

Afterwards, I stared at the ceiling thinking about Joel. I felt so bad that I got up and typed this letter:

> *Dear Joel:*
> *I agree with you that I am a selfish monster who has been a really dismal friend to you. You did not deserve that. You have been wonderful and supportive toward me. If my behavior in any way led to you having to go back into the hospital then I think I will die of guilt. Please forgive me. As soon as you are out of the hospital or are allowed to make phone calls or send emails, please contact me asap. I have so much to tell you about. So many changes. I am in therapy again. I know I can be a better person.*
> *Love, K*

I printed it out then folded it up and slipped it inside one of my mom's Christmas cards, which are navy blue with a big white snowflake (the same card that killed my dad). Even though Joel is Jewish I decided it was okay to give it to him because snow is universal and Christmas is a happy time of the year no matter what religion you are. Even though the doctor said to take it easy, I walked to the corner and mailed the card so that Joel will get it soon. Now I can go to sleep knowing I did at least one good thing in my life.

Oh, I emailed Margaret and told her I was still not allowed to put weight on my ankle yet, and that I would not be back to work until Monday. This gives me a few days to build up my courage.

Thursday, April 17, 2008

Thank you for all the kind letters saying I did the correct thing getting an abortion and that it would have been selfish of me to bring a baby into the world when I am so clearly not ready. And fuck you to everyone who wrote to tell me I'm a cold-blooded killer. Especially the little girl in Florida who says she can hardly sleep she is so worried about my eternal soul. You know what, honey? Grow some pubes then worry about others.

Friday, April 18, 2008

When I woke up, there was a very intense, weird message from Joel Seidler. He got home from the hospital this morning and he is enraged at me for not writing to him after his mom told me what happened. He obviously didn't get my letter. I will wait a few days until the hospital forwards it to him. Once he reads it I am sure he will feel terrible and apologize for being such a dick.

Saturday, April 19, 2008

Paj2453 sent me a poem to cheer me up. I don't know if he wrote it himself or he got it from a book but I like it very much.

THERE IS SUCH LOVE

There is such love that does no harm,
Leaves no one choking in its wake.
No one's sanity is torn in two
Or sacrificed for fealty's sake.
Its calm is deep, its sleep is sound,
Misgivings never quake and size.
It does not reveal its opposite
Or make a separate peace with lies.
It draws no pint, breaks no bones,
Lays waste to nothing in the chest:
Of all loves I've never known,
Surely this one is the best.

It reminds me that almost all love is crazy and painful so I shouldn't beat myself up for loving Paul so deeply. Will I be strong enough to bid him farewell forever?

Sunday, April 20, 2008

This morning I called Glenn and told him how scared I was to call the Spooners and quit. I said Paul was going to be crushed. Glenn insisted that I was wrong, that when a man in his forties is cheating on his wife with a teenage girl, no matter how much he cares about her, a part of him will always be relieved when it's over, because he knows he has played a dangerous game and that he is lucky to have gotten out alive. It was hard for me to picture Paul being relieved that he will never make love to me again.

Tomorrow is Monday. Even though it would be breaking my promise to Glenn, I could go into work tomorrow and then, when we are alone together, tell Paul in person. No, bad idea. If I see him, I will melt and everything will be out of control again. I will do it tonight. On the phone.

The other scary conversation is going to be telling my mom that I am moving into the garage of an ex-rapist. She will have a fit. But once she meets Glenn, I think she will see what a wonderful man he is. He is not at all the same person who committed that heinous crime. He said I can come over to his house any time I want to see my new garage apartment. Maybe tomorrow.

· · ·

To give you an idea of how much I trust Glenn, he is the only person in the world I have told about my blog. I thought he would be really impressed because it is a literary achievement (I think so) but he said that even though he admires my commitment to it, he dislikes blogging. He thinks it's marvelous to keep a diary or journal, but that there's something dishonest about showing it to the world. He said our whole culture is way too desperate for attention. We're all famous in our own minds. I had to laugh because I have always felt I was going to be famous for something someday. I just didn't know what. I was waiting to be discovered. Ha!

Now that I am about to move into my first apartment, I realize how badly I have needed to be on my own, living apart from my mom. It's time for me to start making my own life decisions.

Moving in with Glenn is going to be like starting over. With a new job. And no boyfriend. And no more alcohol or drugs. (Since I have to attend three AA meetings, I might as well quit for a while and see how it feels, right?) This is my chance to be a better person. Maybe it's a good time to stop blogging. Just see what it's like to live without describing and analyzing everything I do. Just live!

. . .

Cancel my reality show. Crazy, huh?

Is Barack Obama correct? Can human beings really dream a whole new life and then make it come true? Or do they eventually turn around and go right back to the way things were?

Paul says there's no such thing as happily ever after and that the world gets worse. Only one way to find out, I guess. Just live! Hahaha!

I will call Paul now.

Wait, phone ringing. Somebody loves me. Stand by.

...

Friday, April 25, 2008

Dear Readers:

My name is Carol Grantham. I am the mother of Amy Grantham, whom you know as Katie Kampenfelt. Five days ago, within an hour of her last entry, at around 7:00 p.m., Amy got in her car, drove away, and never returned. She has not been seen or heard from since.

Everyone who loves Amy is sick with worry. Local police, as well as a private detective whom I have hired, are currently investigating her disappearance. We know very little so far except that Amy has not withdrawn any money from her bank account, used her cell phone, or attempted to use her credit card, which was given to her for emergencies.

Like many young women, Amy is imaginative to the extreme, as well as enormously secretive. In this blog she changed not only her own name but the names of everyone with whom she came into contact. This has made the investigation of her disappearance difficult.

If any of you exchanged e-mails or phone calls with Amy in which she confided anything that might help us to locate her, please write to me at this website. I am offering a $25,000 reward for any information that leads to the discovery of her whereabouts.

No matter what you think of my daughter, I can assure you that she is a wonderful girl. A person of remarkable spirit, intelligence, humor, beauty, and courage. If you know anything that might help us to find her, please contact me at once.
Yours truly, Carol Grantham

Friday, May 2, 2008

Dear Readers:
First, let me thank you for your letters of support. I know that Amy would be touched by your outpouring of concern. To those of you who write only to inflict pain, I beg you to stop. Please show some compassion.

In the week since I last wrote to you, a great deal of time has been devoted to questioning each and every person mentioned in this blog, in the hopes that one or more of them might hold the key to Amy's disappearance. We began with the people who knew her best. It was not difficult to find the boy whom you know as Rory. Amy's boyfriend has been a fixture in our home, on and off, since they began dating last year. We know from a review of Amy's phone records that the call which Amy received while posting her final blog was from him. We were curious as to whether he would tell us this fact without being prompted. He did. He said that he called her the night she disappeared to apologize for his angry outburst. He claims that while he had lost his temper with her on many occasions, he has never shaken or struck her. He confirmed his affair with "Jade." Our investigator asked how long they had spoken on that final night and he said ten minutes. Phone records show that, in reality, they spoke for thirty-eight. It remains to be seen if this discrepancy is meaningful.

This phone call was not, in fact, Amy's last. Phone records show that two minutes after she hung up with Rory, she received another call on her landline, this one from a blocked caller. The call lasted less than two minutes. Approximately ten minutes later, Amy left the house without saying good-bye. Who placed this final phone call? Why did Amy leave the house in such a hurry?

Our investigator could find no one in the area teaching film history who matched the description or particulars of "Dan

Gallo." Through a combination of good police work and blind luck, we eventually discovered the real Dan, who is the day manager of a local video store.

Given a chance to read Amy's blog for the first time, he confirmed that the substance of their relationship as described was true, but he claimed never to have received a phone call from her about the possibility that he might be the father of her unborn child. He said that if he had, he would not have hung up on her. He said that the last time they spoke was five or six nights before her disappearance when she called him at work. He had told her many times never to call him there. Annoyed, he told her that he would call her back as soon as he could. He never did.

The local couple who hired Amy to be their nanny, the "Spooners," confirm all of the facts of this blog except the most important one. The husband denies any improper sexual relations with Amy. We have no way of disputing this. We are urging local authorities to obtain a search warrant.

Amy's former tutor, "Joel Seidler," was not difficult to find, as Amy did not bother to change his last name. He says that her disappearance has devastated him. He is also burdened by a terrible feeling of guilt, because their last contact (the voice mail he left) was so unfriendly. His mother claims that he has never shown a history of violence toward anyone but himself.

Our investigator spoke to "Jade," but found her in a very bad state due to obvious drug abuse. She confirmed that she and

Amy had not been in contact for months, but denied ever having had a sexual or romantic relationship with Rory.

We still have not been able to track down "Nick Dempster." On each day that Amy claims he left her a voice mail, she did indeed receive at least one phone call from a blocked caller ID. Is this the same blocked caller who contacted Amy the night she disappeared? We have no way of knowing.

Which brings us to "Glenn A. Warburg." While he confirms the truth of all of the early incidents Amy relates, he claims that he never saw or spoke to her again after she left his employ. Which would mean that everything which took place afterwards was a complete fabrication. We have found no record of Amy having received an abortion under her own name at any clinic within two hundred miles of here. While Mr. Warburg's home has no free-standing garage, there is an empty guest bedroom.

I beg you once more for your help. If any of you exchanged e-mails or phone calls with Amy in which she confided anything that might shed some light on her whereabouts, please write to me here. Your help will be kept strictly confidential. There is now a $50,000 reward for any information leading to the discovery of Amy. Again thank you for your prayers and good wishes.

Yours truly, Carol Grantham

p.s. To those of you who continue to send hateful and threatening e-mails filled with contempt for my daughter and ridicule of me, I beg you once again to stop. From now on your letters will be turned over to the police.

Friday, May 9, 2008

Dear Readers:

Again I want to thank those of you who have taken the time to write to me, not only to express sympathy and genuine concern but to offer help. I cannot tell how much I appreciate it. While most of your help so far has been in the form of conjecture and speculation (much of it quite shrewd), we are still hopeful that one of you might have something more concrete to offer.

Many of you have written with suspicions in regard to the man you know as "Mr. Silaggi." In the days after Amy's disappearance, I called the last phone number I had for the "Silaggis" and there was no answer. Yesterday our investigator tracked them down to a retirement community in Green Valley, Arizona. I just hung up with their daughter and would like to share with you what I have learned.

Amy's letter was forwarded to them in Arizona. Since "Mr. Silaggi" is legally blind and no longer reads his own mail, his wife (I will call her "Elsa") read it aloud to him. Needless to say, she was appalled. "Mr. Silaggi" denied Amy's allegations, insisting that she was either crazy or a liar or both. This might very well have been the end of it, except that Elsa had the good sense to call their daughter and tell her of Amy's accusations.

Elsa's daughter (whom I have met just once or twice) called me tonight to say that she believes Amy's accusations. In fact, she is certain they are true. She only wishes that she herself had shown such courage.

I doubt that "Mr. Silaggi" had anything to do with the disappearance of my daughter, but I am proud that Amy had the strength of character to confront him. I am sorry that she had to go through this trauma alone. I wish she had come to me.
Yours truly, Carol Grantham

Monday, May 11, 2008

This morning the decomposed remains of a young female were discovered a hundred miles away, in a stream at a local forest preserve. Amy's dental records are on their way to the coroner's office.

Pray there is no match.

Since Amy's disappearance, on nights when I cannot sleep, I read and reread this blog. I read your letters, even the cruelest ones. I ask myself who would want to hurt my daughter. I hear the answer: almost anyone.

Amy is my heart, my whole life. I cannot imagine that I will never see her again.